HOW OFTEN WE COLLIDE

MADELINE FLAGEL

Madeline Flagel

madelineflagelauthor@gmail.com

ISBN: 979-8-9878295-2-3 (paperback edition)

ISBN: 979-8-9878295-1-6 (ebook edition)

Cover Design by Rachel McEwan, Rachel McEwan Designs

Editing by Paige Lawson

Published February 2023

Published by Madeline Flagel

CONTENT WARNING

Content Warning: this book contains explicit sexual content

To my sister, this is for you. Thank you for always believing in me, in literally everything I've ever done. And for putting up with my annoying ass for thirty-one years.

Love, Pooh

CHAPTER ONE

"Viv, what in the hell are you going to do?"

"I'll take a vodka soda with two limes, please," I call to the waiter, completely ignoring Lauren.

We've been sitting at this bar for three full minutes, and she's already pressing me about getting fired today. It's not my fault, anyways. I mean, not *totally* my fault.

"Lauren, the man screamed in my face. You know me. Was I just supposed to just take it?"

"I mean, yes. I don't like everything that happens at my job, but I have to pay my bills."

"Well, I'm not you. I'm not perf—," I stop myself and swallow down the word.

I'm visibly irritated and finding it hard to keep the frustration from pulling at my features. I don't want to be rude to Lauren; she's only worried about me. And she has a hundred reasons why she should be.

I have no job and bills to pay — something I should have thought about earlier today. I'm twenty-four with no boyfriend or any prospects, for that matter. Don't even get me started on the degree my parents paid for that I have yet to use.

I mean, the list could go on...but, whatever the reason, I'm being too hard on her. She is the only person who has been there for me since I moved to Boston. So, maybe I don't have much, but I at least have her.

"I'm sorry. Lauren I—" as I'm getting ready to start my apology tour with her, the waiter comes back with our drinks.

Thank god.

"No, I get it," Lauren says as her eyes drop. "It's the Anniversary, isn't it? Of your mom's death?"

"That has nothing to do with what happened," I lie, not sounding convincing in the least because Lauren's eyes narrow right into mine.

"Just promise me you're going to get out and look for another job. I just worry for you. I love you and want you to be happy and not homeless..." Lauren trails off.

"I'm fine, Lo. Plus, I need a better job. Something that makes sense for the dream."

"The bookstore dream?"

"Yes. A place that's mine, with all my favorite books...that smells like coffee and worn pages."

"But you need something now, Viv. At least until dreams start paying us."

"I still have some of what my dad left me, and my apartment is paid through the year. Can we just relax tonight? It's been a long day."

I don't feel like going into detail with Lauren about how the inheritance my dad left me when he died is painfully running out at lightning speed. It's not that I'm foolish with my money. It's just, well..it wasn't a lot, to begin with. It was enough to sustain me living in a decent apartment for six years. It was enough to let me not work my first year to focus on school, and it was enough to buy my car. The problem is, it's not enough anymore. And I'm screwed if I don't get another job, and quickly for that matter. But I'm not telling her that. Despite being older by almost nine months, she acts like a Mom, hovering and protecting me.

Lauren is really my only family, and not just in Boston. We met in economics class— she sat in the front row, and when I was late to my first day, the only available seat was the one right next to hers. She had her long blonde hair pulled up with her ponytail in soft curls and wore a white sweater and red lipstick. She looked like an actress, and I remember wondering why the hell she was there and not on a movie set with George Clooney. She was the first person to talk to me, the first person to show me around campus. She invited me to a party at her dorm that night, and since then, there haven't been many days where we've been apart.

"How did your date with Pete go?" She asks, switching to another awful topic.

"Miserable," I say with a disgusted look on my face. "He chewed with his mouth open the entire time, not to mention he spoke while he was eating. I can look past many things, but nothing in this world pisses me off more than hearing someone munch away on their dinner." I shudder at the memory.

Lauren laughs, but it's true. I'm hard to please, and maybe I'm too picky, but I have a right to be. My dad set high expectations for me regarding what qualities to look for in a man. My father was kind and gentle — he worshiped the ground my mother walked on. He also didn't chew with his mouth open.

It's not that much to ask, is it?

"I'm done going on dates for a long time," I say as I raise my glass. I continue to sip my drink while asking Lauren how Carter is.

"Carter is Carter," she replies with a familiar blush, and so often, I'm envious of it.

They have been dating for two years, and I'm just waiting for the day he proposes. He's great for her and understands the relationship she and I have. Some nights we will have sleepovers while Carter stays at their house alone. He doesn't intend to take away our friendship, and I appreciate that. I appreciate him.

"Jesus Christ," Lauren says as she rolls her eyes. I stop and listen, and sure enough...karaoke is starting.

"Remember when I said nothing in this world pisses me off more than hearing someone chew?" I say, smiling at Lauren.

Karaoke is the one thing that will draw us out of a bar faster than anything else. It's not that I hate people who want to pursue their dreams of singing, I just hate live music and drunk people screaming into microphones.

"Let's get out of here. I better get to bed if I want to get up bright and early and apply for jobs," I say to her with a wink, completely faking my enthusiasm.

We cash out our tab and head for the door. With long-winded goodbyes, we always make sure to say *I love you* and *text me when you're home*.

The sharp air hits my lungs while I watch Lauren get into her car and drive off, and I struggle to get the keys out of my purse, flustered from the day. When I finally find them, I slip inside and lean my body onto my passenger seat, resting my head on it and taking a deep breath through my nose, only to calm my irritation. I didn't mean to screw up that guy's coffee, but did he really have to scream at me and berate me like I was a child? No, no, he didn't. That's why I got loud. Unfortunately, my boss is a firm believer that the customer is always right.

What a crock of shit.

I sit upright and back out of the parking lot. The rain buckets down as I drive, and my eyes focus on the traffic while my head is still stuck in today's events. Maybe I should have just taken it? I mean, it was one customer. Coming up to the intersection near my apartment, my phone dings.

Lauren: Made it home. Good luck tomorrow!

I click the side of my phone to shut off the bright light that glows in the darkness of my car when I'm suddenly jolted. My head hits the window to the left of me in an instant, and a loud crack follows. The sound of tires screeching is all I hear as a sharp pain pierces through my head, and a veil of darkness washes over me.

As I'm coming to, I can hear the rain falling. The sound of it pelting to the ground is almost peaceful. I try to listen longer before hearing a man's faint voice, but dear god, my head hurts. He's becoming louder and louder, and I just want him to be *quiet*. I try to open my eyes, but the pain in my head is unbearable—a pounding rhythm with my heartbeat. I somehow feel it'll hurt less if I keep my eyes shut, so I do just that.

"Hello! Miss, can you hear me?" A deep voice yells. Why won't he shut up? He's making my head feel even worse.

After a while, I don't hear him, so I stay still. I don't know what happened, and I'm not ready to find out. I was in the car...then what?

I'm just trying to get my head to stop throbbing by taking in slow, deep breaths in hopes that it will solve it. I hear the voice again, "Miss, are you ok?"

I start to open my eyes because, *hopefully*, that will shut him up. I tilt my body up as much as possible but wince in pain because that movement alone makes my head feel even worse. I open my eyes further to see that there is no glass in my driver's side window, causing the rain to seep in. I can make out a figure too, but it's a blur.

"Stay with me," the voice demands.

"It's not like I'm going anywhere," I mutter with a groan, and at that moment, it dawns on me...*I've been in an accident.*

Christ, did I cause it because I was looking at my phone? How bad am I hurt? I can't feel anything besides this overwhelming pounding in my skull. My ears are ringing, and I feel nauseous. I groan as I open my eyes again to see the man with his hands on the roof of my car. He peers into my driver-side window, *or lack thereof*, and I can see he's bleeding, although I can't tell from where. Maybe his voice added to the pounding in my head, but his blazing chocolate eyes send warmth coursing through my whole body. I feel safer — calmer when he looks at me.

I must be dead. This is the kind of man they only make in heaven. *Am I in heaven*? My parents would be so proud. I'm surprised, though. I was almost positive I was going straight to hell for all the shit I've done in my little twenty-four years of life.

Between the numerous one-night stands and the underage drinking, there was a strong possibility Satan, and I were going to be very close when that time came.

"There you are," he says with a half smile as if trying to keep me entertained long enough to keep my eyes open. "My name is Matt. You were in a pretty bad accident.

We've got help coming. Can you tell me what your name is?"

Why do I feel like he's playing twenty questions with me, and how can I get him to stop talking? I realize he's not yelling, but his voice is stinging my ears. As I start to speak, I can feel something warm falling from my chin, I don't think I'm crying, but it feels like tears, hundreds of them.

I blink and realize these tears are going into my eyes. It stings, and it's thick like molasses. Falling into my mouth, I can taste it—it's not tears, it's blood and a lot of it. I try to wipe my left eye with my hand while telling him my name, except my hand feels heavy, like I just ran a ten-mile marathon and can hardly crawl to the finish line.

"Vivian," I get out with an exasperated sigh, finally getting my hand high enough to wipe the blood from my eye. I'm so tired, *why* am I tired, is my brain giving out? Is *this* how I die?

I slowly sit my body up as much as possible, groaning as I lift my chest to make my posture straighter. I look around. *My poor car*. It's totaled. The passenger side is completely crushed. My windshield, or what's left of it, is shattered. Glass is on the dash, on my lap, everywhere...there's glass *everywhere,* and the pounding in my head grows stronger by the second.

I look to my left to see the man still standing by my driver's side door.

"Are you ok?" I manage to mutter to him in what little breath I have. I can see he's bleeding just above his eyebrow and take note of how thick, almost manicured, his eyebrows actually are.

"I'm fine," he says with his lips pressed hard together, "You were t-boned, and your car slammed into mine." His voice is laced with sympathy, but I can see the angst in his eyes. The way he's looking at me like I should be dead right now.

I don't get to say anything else before my eyes draw heavy, closing on their own at the same time my mind grows completely silent.

CHAPTER TWO

The faint sounds of sirens are ringing in my ears as I regain consciousness and feel pressure as my body is lifted. It seems my ears are plugged because I can't make out any words, just different sets of muffled voices. I feel like I'm in someone's arms, but I'm too weak to hold on.

A low groan comes out of my mouth as I try to lift my heavy eyelids. I can now see that the tall man by my car is carrying me in his arms. I feel like I'm as light as a feather, the way he holds me is strong and secure to his body.

I'm trying to gather my thoughts on my brief conversation with him, but my mind is drawing a blank. I can't think of anything except that my head is now surging with pain again, so I spring open my eyes and start to weep. Crying only worsens as a new stabbing pain shoots under my chest, and I try to clutch my body — still too weak to move.

"Dr. Halloway, you need to be looked at too. Set her down on this gurney so we can clean you up," I can clearly hear another man's voice say.

I get placed carefully on something hard, finally able to bring my hands to the top of my ribs as I wail out in pain again.

Three EMTs rush to me as I go in and out of consciousness. I've never been in an accident before, and it took me a long time to get into a car after my mother's death. That dreadful feeling of not knowing what happened but realizing something awful has plagues my mind. And suddenly, I'm back at her funeral, considering how short life is and wondering when my time is up.

When I open my eyes again, they are closing the ambulance doors. I'm strapped in with a woman to my right spouting something off about medicine as she pulls back a rather large syringe of something I know will be injected inside me. To my left is a figure that I try to make out before my eyes shut again.

"Yes, Mass Gen, tell Dr. Lundy to call CT," He says.

I smile at that familiar voice. My pain is gone, I can't feel anything anymore, and I don't know if that's a good sign or a bad one, but for some odd reason, I feel a hell of a lot better with him here.

"What's your name again?" I say loudly, faintly pointing in his direction, but my words come out slurred, like I'm intoxicated.

"Matthew," he says with a light laugh and probably the most contagious smile I've ever seen. "We're going to Mass Gen right now, and we will have you looked at. You have a pretty bad laceration by your hairline, and we want to make sure you don't have a brain bleed or any other internal injuries."

He keeps saying *we*. Why is he coming too? I mean, truthfully, I don't care. I kind of never want him to leave my side again, but isn't it kind of weird to be riding in the same ambulance? Couldn't he have caught his own? How are the EMTs allowing this? I've never been in the back of an ambulance, but I just know my dad couldn't ride in the back with my mom when he arrived on the scene. He had to follow behind. If they wouldn't let my dad tag along for the ride, how in the hell are they letting this random man?

I don't question it anymore. I'm feeling great, and I'm alive. I should be thankful. I still haven't texted Lauren that I was home, though.

Shit.

"Lauren!" I shout as I try to sit up, but they have me strapped in this thing like a deranged patient. "I need my phone. I need my phone now," I say frantically.

"I couldn't find it, I tried to grab any belongings you had in the car, but it was so destroyed, I couldn't really see anything," Matthew says.

"I need to call my friend. Do you have a phone? She's probably worried sick. I should have been home by now. She will know something is wrong."

"They'll notify your family when you get to the hospital, I promise."

"You don't understand; I don't have anyone else. I need to get ahold of her right now."

Just as I'm telling Matthew her phone number, we come to a halt, and the doors swing open. It's a short time before I'm whisked out of the back of the ambulance and into the hospital, with Matthew following behind. Seeing him in the light gives me a clearer view. His hair is dark brown, almost black. It's shorter on the sides with a medium length on top, and the stubble on the lower part of his face highlights his sharp jawline. He's wearing dark blue jeans that seem to fit him perfectly and a black long-sleeve shirt that hugs tight around his arms. I can see now what looks like a Steri-Strip right by his eyebrow, but it's hard to tell as we get further away.

"Call her, *please!*" I yell, hoping I finished giving the entirety of the number before we part. They rush me down the hall, and whatever medicine they gave me is in full effect. My eyes are so heavy and tired that I have no choice but to close them.

———*ele*———

*Beep...beep...beep...*is the only thing filling my ears as I open my eyes again. I faintly remember going in and out of machines, *a lot* of people's eyes on me, and *even more* questions. The questions were simple enough, though. *What's your name? How old are you? Where were you traveling to?* I think I answered them all correctly, but I can't even try to form a thought before the door to my room swings open.

"Oh, thank *God,*" Lauren says as she bursts into my room with pink flowers wrapped in something that resembles butcher paper. I give a gentle smile, still feeling pretty weak.

The sun is beaming through the windows, and I can feel the warmth on the right side of my body.

It's morning already? What happened?

"How long have I been out?" I ask quietly.

"Just the night. They gave you some pretty strong meds. Some hot doc said you were screaming and crying, so they gave you the really good stuff."

"Really good stuff," I mutter. I let the muscles in my shoulders ease from their tense state but then perk up again. "Hot doc?"

"Yes, Viv, you don't remember?" She answers.

"I think I would remember a hot doctor, Lo." I giggle, but the pain sears through my ribcage like fire.

As I'm about to ask her what the doctor's name is, a soft knock taps on the door. In usual medical staff fashion, we say nothing before it swings open.

"Vivian! I'm so happy to see you awake, and you have a visitor!" The nurse says excitedly, her cheeks swell to her eyes with how big her grin is.

God, I wish I remembered this lady. She seems happy to see me.

"How are you feeling, sweetie?" She looks me over and then shifts her gaze to Lauren. "This girl had us cracking up back and forth from her scans," she says, pointing at me. "I'm going to page Dr. Halloway. He wanted to know the second you woke up. I'll be right back. Need anything, kiddo?"

"No, thank you," I say quietly with a pressed smile. I glance over at Lo to see her dialing on her phone, bringing it to her ear as it rings.

"Hey, babe! She's awake....yeah...uh hu...ok," she points to the door and glances at me while she mouths what looks to be like *I'll be right outside,* but her red lipstick is so bright, and the way the sun is shining on her, it's hard to tell.

She exits my room, and I take in my surroundings. The flowers Lauren brought me are resting on a table near my head. The hospital room is pretty plain. Four walls, one window, and a heap of machines beeping. I glance at the nurse's station next to me and spot a cup with the writing *Massachusetts General Hospital* embossed on the side, and a feeling of dread seeps in. This is where they brought my mother's body. Where they worked on her for hours only to tell my dad, who was pacing the halls where Lauren stands, that his wife — his soulmate, was gone.

I hate thinking about this. Grief is a weird thing. It consumes me one minute, then the next, I'm completely fine.

I grew up in Chicago, but my parents always traveled for my mom's work. Once my dad retired, he was free to follow along with her, and he gladly did so. Her job brought her to Boston frequently, and they would always come back home ranting and raving about the cuisine, the experience, and all the sightseeing they did. It piqued my curiosity enough to make me want to apply to college here.

On my mom's last work trip, she was hit by a drunk driver. Medics said she died on the scene, but my dad swore he saw her breathing. Regardless, by the time she arrived here, at the same hospital I'm at, they did what they could for a solid two hours before pronouncing her dead.

It took my father a long time to travel again. I don't think he ever was quite the same after that. Sure, he had me, and he told me how grateful he was for that every day. We grew so close that by the time he passed away, I felt like my heart and soul went with him. Not only did I lose my father, but I also lost my best friend. The absolute best friend a girl could ask for.

That feeling of losing them both is as if someone took a dull knife, looked me dead in the eyes, and slowly pressed it through my skin, right in the center of my heart. Then twisted, and twisted, until it finally broke flesh and pushed through slowly until that breaking pain became unbearable, and I had no choice but to scream with everything I had to make it stop.

Of course, I was *devastated* when my mom died, but I was twelve, and I had a lot more anger for the driver that hit her and ran than sadness in my heart. My dad passed when I was seventeen, giving us five years of just him and me.

There's that grief; it comes at me in waves.

As a tear falls from my cheek at the remembrance of both of them, my body reacts in a slight jerk from the knocking at the door. As it is pushed open, I see a very *familiar* tall figure. Only this time, he is wearing dark blue scrubs and a stethoscope around his neck.

"Vivian, " he says excitedly with that beaming smile of his. I'm sure I look like a buffoon at this point, awkwardly gawking at him like this isn't the same man from the accident.

"Hi, *doctor*?" I say, confused.

"Ha, yes. That's me. How are you feeling? Can I get you anything?"

Why is everyone asking if I need something? It's to the point I feel like I *should* ask for something.

"Can I have some water?"

"Absolutely." He nods. "Do you remember anything from last night?"

I tell him the bits and pieces I *do* remember, which isn't much.

"It was pretty bad. You're lucky to be alive. We were both going through the intersection at the same time when you got t-boned directly on your passenger side. It sent your car spinning, crashing into mine."

"Oh my god, I'm so sorry," I exclaim, covering my hands over my mouth.

"You don't have to be sorry, Vivian, it wasn't your fault, and even if it was, I wouldn't be mad at you. People make mistakes. It's human nature. Let me go get you that water. I'll be right back." He lifts off the side of my bed, heading for the door again.

'Hot' isn't the word to describe this man. He's *magnificent*. I'm completely enamored looking at him. If Aphrodite and Adonis had a human child, it would be him.

Just as quickly as he left, he reappears with a small styrofoam cup of water for me.

"How long do I have to stay here?" I ask as he hands me my cup while taking a seat on the edge of my bed.

"Just until this afternoon. Imaging showed you have a couple of cracked ribs, but your lungs look clear. At this point, we don't believe you need surgery."

"Oh," I interject, absorbing the information.

"You'll have to take it easy for about three to five weeks. Do you have someone at home to help you recover?"

"No, it's just me...but I can see if my friend can help," I reply. Selfishly, I'm hoping he's asking me if I have anyone at home to see if I have a spouse or something of that nature, but I know it's a general question he probably has to ask. A girl can dream, though. "Shouldn't you be *not* working right now? Since, ya know, I rammed my car into yours," I say, lifting my finger to point at his butterfly stitches.

"I'm fine," he says sweetly with that damned smile. "I didn't want anyone else taking care of you. I've seen some horrific things, and to be honest, the way you looked in that car...I didn't think...I didn't think you would make it, let alone have minor injuries for what it was," he says while rubbing the top of his head.

God, his *hair* looks so soft. I can't stop my mind from thinking about what it would feel like to run my fingers through it.

"Well, I appreciate it, Matt," I say. "I'm sorry, Doctor..." I trail off, already forgetting his last name.

"Doctor Halloway, but Matt is just fine," he says with his lips curled in a pressed smile. I like this smile too, but his big grin is the best one by far. Just as I'm gazing into his eyes, Lauren enters the room along with the friendly nurse.

"Vivian, we are getting your papers ready for discharge. Dr. Lundy will be in here to go over your homework," the sweet nurse says.

"Homework?" I ask curiously.

"Yes, Hunny, a lot of rest, some breathing exercises, and a couple of other things. Do you have someone at home to help you move about?"

"I-" I start to say before getting cut off by Lauren. "Yes, I'll be staying with her for as long as she needs," she blurts out.

"Great!" the nurse says. "Dr. Halloway, the patient in room 113 is requesting Dilaudid again," she explains with a concerned look on her.

"I'll be right there," he says.

"Vivian, I'll be back before you leave, " he explains while lifting again off my bed.

I smile and give him a quick nod.

My eyes follow them out, hoping by pressing my stare, they'll move faster. I've been praying everyone would get out of my room quickly because that bathroom here has been calling my name since I opened my eyes.

"Lo, help me...please," I struggle to sit up even straighter as she grabs my arm to help lift me. I cry out in pain. Whatever movement we are trying to do to get me off this bed is hurting even worse.

"Let's try this," Lauren says as she swings my legs over the side of the bed. "Bathroom?"

Damn, she knows me so well.

As we slowly make our way to the bathroom, I can't help but hold my hand on the part of my ribs that hurt. I'm trying to move as fast as I can but being hunched over in pain is making me walk at turtle speed.

Lauren helps me to the toilet, but I tell her I can take it from here and will let her know when I'm finished. I love her, but I'm not about to have her stare at me while I piss. Only a moment of relief passes before I get back up slowly, holding the railing to my right. I waddle to the sink and place both hands on the sides of it as I lift my head into the mirror.

"What in the *fuck!*" I yell loud enough for Lauren to rush in.

My head is bandaged, and the hair under it is matted and clumped with dried blood. You can't even tell my hair *was* a shiny chocolate color. It looks dull, lifeless, and tinged with maroon compared to how I left that bar. Whatever makeup I had on last night is gone, and my bottom lip is swollen — dried blood hovers the opening of a cut that slices through the center of it. Around my head wrap, I can see bruising that stretches all the way under my left eye.

I look like I boxed Floyd Mayweather and *lost*.

"I look like...*THIS?!*" I wail to Lauren, looking at her through the mirror.

"Christ, Viv, I thought you fell!"

"Lauren, please tell me this is a fucking joke," I squeal back

"Viv, stop. You literally got into a *car accident*."

"The only time that doctor has seen me is when I look like *this*!"

I know I'm lucky to be alive, but I would have at least hoped I looked a little better during it all. Or that someone could have at least run a comb through my hair.

"We have to go. Now." I demand Lauren.

Thankfully, only another forty minutes pass before Dr. Lundy finishes reviewing my discharge papers, but I notice Dr. Halloway still hasn't returned. I'm a little glad because of my appearance, but I was really hoping he would at least say goodbye. I'm ready to be home, though, so the best I can do is write *Thanks Doc* on a napkin and leave it on my bedside table, hoping it will reach him so I can express some kind of gratitude for him being there with me since the very beginning.

Lauren helps me get dressed — in the same bloody clothes I came in here with and positions me comfortably in the wheelchair before we're off. Down the halls, in an elevator, then out the door.

"Carter said he's going to bring us chipotle when he gets off work," she says excitedly.

"Ok, good. Is it too late to ask for extra guac?"

"I already did." She gives me a sly smile. "So...did ya get his number?"

"Who? The doctor?" I say with a twisted expression.

"Yes, Viv..the doctor. What a hotty." *I don't know why she keeps calling him hot. I swear that doesn't do him any justice.*

"No, I didn't get his number. I wasn't about to ask, either. He's a doctor...they basically have their entire lives figured out. I'm sure he's married with kids, and how awkward would that be for me to ask him? He was just doing his job by helping me. He was just doing his job by checking in on me. He was just doing his job, Lo," I ramble on, not sure if I'm trying to convince her or myself at this point.

"Ok, Ok, Vivian...don't get your panties in a bunch." She laughs.

"Besides, I look like *ass*. At least let me ask him when I'm somewhat put together," I say back with a smile. Knowing damn well I may never see that man again, and *her* knowing damn well I'm not forward enough to ever do something like that anyways.

CHAPTER THREE

Pulling up to my apartment, I'm starting to realize how incredibly difficult moving about is going to be for me during these next five weeks. There are at least seven steps to walk up just to get to my front door. My bedroom is upstairs, but thankfully, there is a guest bedroom on the main floor, so that's where I'll be staying for a while. The thought of climbing any stairs is making me nauseous, or maybe it's the pain meds we just picked up from the pharmacy.

Lauren luckily finds a parking spot right in front, and once she gets out and opens my door, I take in what I'm looking at. Leaves are bustling with the wind; they range in color from green to that slight tinge of burnt orange on some of the edges. The air is crisp, and the sky is faintly saturated with grey as if rain is coming soon. The breeze isn't too cold, though. It's refreshing.

I'm happy to be here; I'm happy to be alive. I was very fortunate to walk away from the accident last night. At least five hospital staff *including* Matt told me so. I glance at Lauren and smile. She's been patiently waiting for me to get out of the car, looking at me with a confused grin.

"I'm thankful," I say out loud to her.

"So am I," she says back with an endearing smile.

She helps me inside, plopping me onto my couch and handing me the remote.

"What can I get from upstairs for you? Carter was going to pick up your new phone on the way to Chipotle. Want him to grab you some diet coke too? It looks like you're out," she yells from the kitchen with the refrigerator door open.

"Yeah, yeah, that all sounds good. Can you just grab as many pajamas as you can find?" I shout back over my shoulder.

After four weeks of me waddling around my house, things are getting a little easier. It still hurts to take a deep breath, but as far as taking care of myself independently, I've got that down pat. I sent Lauren home after the first week when I was able to get out of bed on my own. I don't want to be a burden, and as selfish as I wanted to be by keeping her here the entire recovery, she has a life at home...with Carter.

It's been absolute hell staying home, though. I've binged watched nearly every show on Netflix, and I can't wait for the moment I'm cleared to run again. I need to get out of the house. Hell, I can't wait for the moment when I can walk a mile just to grab a coffee. I'm not myself when I'm stuck at home. I'm at my happiest when I'm productive, achieving something day to day. The only thing I've been achieving these past weeks is lifting the remote to skip the intro on my shows.

I got that from my mother, I think. She could never sit down; she always had to be up and on the go. I feel useless just lying around, but I know it's exactly what I should be doing. If I push it too much, my recovery will be even longer. At least, that's what my physical therapist said.

As I'm making a sandwich, my phone chimes from the living room.

Lauren: Did you see that Birch Books is hiring?

I did, and I already submitted my application online. She'll be happy to know that, I'm sure.

Owning my own bookstore one day has always been my life's goal, so it wouldn't hurt to get first-hand experience working in one. I'm just a little more realistic when it comes to *big dreams*. I probably will never have the money to fund something like that, and I'm not thinking negatively. It's just the facts. Sure, I could have used my inheritance and bought a small building to start it up, but where would that leave me? Living inside of it? Sleeping on the floor? I don't even think I could *find* a building for that cheap anyways. Ever since I graduated college, I've been saving, and the way it's looking so far...I'll have my own store front when I'm around eighty.

Lucky me.

I finish eating my lunch and respond to Lo.

Me: I did, and I already submitted my app

Lauren: Yay! Hopefully, they call you. How are you feeling?

Me: All good, thanks! Are you free later? Want to get takeout and watch reruns of friends?

Lauren: Be there at 7!

As I change into my pajamas, I take a look at myself in the mirror, brushing the hair out of my eyes and grazing over my scar. It frames my face and isn't noticeable at all when I blow dry my bangs, and for that — I'm thankful.

I still think about that night and replay different scenarios over and over in my head. Had I not fumbled with my keys, I would have been five seconds earlier to that intersection, and the person flying through their red light might have missed me. The police said that the driver was arguing on the phone and going forty over the speed limit, blasting through the stop light. The driver of that vehicle didn't make it, and I can't help but feel somewhat responsible. Had I not been there, though, they still would have hit Matthew. Oh, *Matthew*. I would be lying if I said I haven't thought about him often. I haven't even bothered to look him up online because I'm entirely convinced he was just in *Doctor Mode,* whisking me away from my car and staying with me during the hospital. After all, it's his duty. I'm pretty sure anyone in the medical field is trained to 'save lives' whenever they can. Isn't that like some written rule? But still, he was holding me so tight, carrying me to help, and my head fit perfectly in the crook of his neck. I can't even finish my thought before my doorbell rings. There's a fifty-fifty chance that it's Lauren or Mr. Changs.

"I got us something!" Lauren proclaims, holding a bottle of Chardonnay.

"Lauren! I can't drink on these pain meds!" I laugh with my gut, feeling a sharp sting on the top of my ribs.

"Fine, more for me. Is my shrimp fried rice here yet?" She replies as she barges in the door, making herself at home.

We sit and eat while we watch Ross Geller get a spray tan on TV, and I'm quickly reminded that I still have a heap of recovery to get through. Belly laughs hurt the worst, but this is my favorite episode. How can I not crack up?

"Carter and I are going to the Hamptons next month. Do you think he's going to propose?" She asks in between episodes.

"Well, he hasn't asked me yet, so I'm going to say probably not," I state firmly with a smile, completely lying through my teeth.

Before my accident, Carter had already told me about his planned surprise. Of course, I cried. I'm happy for her, happy for *them*. But it almost makes me feel worse about myself thinking about how far off in life I am. It's like I'm living one day at a time, and the next thing I know — I'm forty-five with no husband, no kids, and a minimum-wage job. I guess. Not that there's anything wrong with that. I just always wanted a big family since mine left this earth too soon. I never got to have any brothers and sisters, so I know what it's like to be alone, and if I ever have one child...three more are going to follow. I want my kids to have each other for the day that maybe I'm not around anymore.

I know I need to not be so picky, *I know* I need to stop with the mindless one-night stands, *I know* what I need to do... it's just easier said than done.

CHAPTER FOUR

When I got a call from Birch Books last week asking for an interview, I immediately called Lo to tell her the news. She was equally excited as I was, but I know never to get my hopes up prematurely. Not until I have something solid, something concrete to be happy for.

I told them about the accident, and without hesitation, they said I could come in whenever my recovery was complete. They already seem nice and desperate for help, which is perfect for me.

Birch Books pays a little more than minimum wage, but honestly, I will take anything at this point. The insurance company gave me a check for my totaled car, and I have zero interest in buying another. I'm not getting behind the wheel for a while. So I just stuck that check right into my savings to put aside for this damn pipe dream of mine.

Thankfully, Birch Books is only six blocks away from my apartment, so if I get this job, I'll be able to walk to work.

Since I'm at the five-week mark, I got cleared from recovery — I'm not one hundred percent better, but it at least doesn't hurt to laugh.

I head upstairs to finish getting ready for my interview. Throwing jean overalls over my white tank, I keep my makeup simple with just mascara and some lip gloss, and thanks to my perfectly dried bangs, my scar isn't noticeable.

I'm not sure if I should try to look more professional or not. It's a book store. Not a receptionist at a law firm like Lauren. I'm fine — *I think*. I head downstairs, cuff the hems of my overalls, and slip on my white Converse shoes before I'm out the door.

Walking down my street, I notice the neighbor kids playing in the park near our homes. I think the smallest one is only five, while his brother seems to be around eight or nine. They give me a quick wave as I pass, and I give them one back.

Walking further, I spot Benny's Cafe, where I used to work. The building is a shit-colored brown, and their coffee is just flavored bean water. I wouldn't order anything from there if someone paid me to.

Fuck Benny's Cafe, and fuck Benny.

I know I'm going to have to tell this book store why I got fired, but I hope when I explain, it doesn't seem so erratic as Benny, my old boss, made it appear.

I get to Birch Books ten minutes early, I may have been a little excited to leave my house today, so I hope they don't mind if I browse what new titles they got in.

Birch Books is on the corner of an intersection, with only the word **Books** written across their black banner in front. Walking through the red door, I can tell it's a small shop, almost crammed with floor-to-ceiling books. It looks pretty disorganized, but what good book store isn't? I can't believe I've only been in here twice since I've lived here, but when you can buy everything online, what's the point of fighting over parking spaces to run in and grab one thing?

I run my fingers along the book spines and take in that familiar scent of smoky paperbacks, almost like the smell of an old attic filled to the brim with soiled pages from everyone's fingertips.

My love for reading started young – but not the romances my mother loved to keep stacked on her shelf. I love mystery, crime, and maybe even some fantasy. I love the escape — I think that's what it is. To be in someone else's world, someone else life. Not dwelling on my own pitiful one.

"Hi, I'm Vivian!" I say with a grin on my face to the older woman behind the counter. "Sorry, I'm a little early."

"No worries, my dear, we're ready for you in the back. My name is Caroline, my husband Bill and I own this shop," she says in a gentle tone.

I can tell she's at least in her late seventies. The creases on her face remind me of the rings underneath the bark of a tree, showing their age gracefully. The laugh lines near the corner of her eyes tell the story of a woman who's smiled for many years, and the sight of it makes me grin even more.

She brings me behind a curtain that's hanging between a book shelf and the register, making our way back through the storage room until we come to an office door. As she opens it, I see a large oak desk with the wall behind it fully covered with shelves that are stacked full of different titles and publications.

My dream office if you ask me.

It's not very big, but the floor-to-ceiling bookshelves make it seem bigger. The older gentleman, who I assume is Bill sits behind the desk.

"Hello, you must be Vivian. Please, have a seat," he says, slowly reaching to shake my hand.

As Caroline and I go to sit on the two chairs facing Bill, I can tell he's much older by the way he moves. He's slow to stand, hunched over for no other reason than his back is probably formed like that with his age. The skin on his hands seems thin, with bruises and a few bandages. As he goes to sit, it's somehow even slower than when he was trying to stand, and I stare in awe at him.

I never met my grandparents, but I would assume they were just like this at some point. My parents were older, so by the time I came along, their parents had already passed. I never got to experience what grandparents were like, but I heard from my friends it was awesome. Cookies and candy all of the time, sleepovers, and home-cooked meals. It fascinated me.

"Tell us a little about yourself, Vivian. Do you go by Vivian, or would you like us to call you something else?" Bill says in a soft tone.

"Vivian or Viv is fine. I go by both," I say with my lips curled in a tight smile. I take a breath and then divulge what little my life is. "Let's see. I've lived in Boston for six years. I'm originally from Chicago.." I hear small gasps from Bill and Caroline both. They look delighted that I mentioned my home town.

I stay smiling for a moment while they take it in. They explain to me how Chicago is where they met forty years ago. It holds a special place in their heart.

We talk about different monuments in Chicago, restaurants that are still there years later, and how so much has changed from forty years ago until now.

"So I see you left your last job pretty hastily, we did call for a reference, and they told us the reason you left, but we want to hear your side first," he says with a more serious look on his face. His eyes drop to the paper in his hands and then back up at me from the tops of his glasses, waiting for me to respond.

I push out a close-mouthed sigh as I get ready to explain. I'm not interested in straying from the truth. I know I wasn't entirely in the wrong, and if they can't see that, then — oh well.

"I had been working there for four years. I never caused any trouble or made any waves. The day I got fired was the anniversary of my mom's passing. Usually, I don't have to work that day, but I was called in by a no-show. I'm not saying this is an excuse at all, though. I woke up already irritated from not getting any sleep which was no one's fault but my own. I worked that shift, then was asked to work a double because the next person didn't come in. I agreed because I need the money, and I would rather be working than sitting at home. We were getting around closing time when a gentleman came in, clearly intoxicated. I could smell the liquor on his breath. He ordered a coffee, and I had apparently made the wrong thing for him. He started yelling and thew his drink on the counter in front of me, covering my shirt and jeans. It was so hot I screamed, and that's when my manager came out to see what the commotion was. The customer continued to call me derogatory names, hounding me like I was a child until, eventually, I had enough and fired back. I called him about every name in the book and told him to leave and never come back. By that time, the manager, staff, and owner were all out from behind the counter, apologizing to the man. As if, he didn't just say those things to me. I got fired on the spot, and if I had the chance to take back anything I said or did — I wouldn't." I let out a long-winded breath.

"Ha!" Bill says after a brief moment of silence, clearly amused. "You go, girl."

"Oh, Hunny, I'm sorry you had to deal with that. I would have told that man to eat shit," Caroline chimes in.

We laugh together, and it feels so nice to actually have someone on my side. I wonder if this is what grandparents are like. They have years of experience on this earth, and I've always found older people to not give a damn anymore. I think that's what I'll be like at that age, less professional, more, *telling people to eat shit.*

We continue to talk about the bookstore, my duties, and what hours they would like me to work. I told them

I would work as many as they possibly could give me. Now that I'm not in school anymore, and my only hobbies include reading and occasionally going for a run, I'm stuck with unlimited free time to make money, which I so desperately need.

Caroline walks me back to the front desk and tells me they will give me a call soon. They have a couple more interviews to get through today first. I thanked them both for their time back in the office but offer another thanks to Caroline as I'm walking out of the door.

I hope they call me back. I really don't want to go to this interview at Fresh Fare, bagging groceries was the only thing they had available, and it pays even less than the book store.

I finally get back home, deciding there is still enough light in the day for a quick run, so I do just that. Knowing I shouldn't press my luck too hard with these ribs, I vow to myself to only do a slight jog.

Somewhere between my house and twelve blocks down the road, I missed a call from an unknown number. Stopping long enough to catch my breath, I call it back.

"Birch Books," the faint voice on the other end says.

"Hi! This is Vivian. I had a missed call."

"Oh, hello, dear! Bill and I wanted to let you know we really loved having you today and were hoping you could start as early as tomorrow."

I haven't even been gone more than an hour and a half. Did they already finish those other interviews?

"We decided to hire you the second you left our store, but we figured we should at least see the other candidates. They were horse shit," she chuckles.

My heart races as a smile sweeps across my face. "I would absolutely love to work for you both. What time do you need me there tomorrow?"

"Ten in the morning would be great dear. We will go over your schedule at that time and see if it's something that works for you. See you then."

I don't know what it is with this woman, but she seems joyous, just full of life. It's hard to explain when you look at her because of her short white hair and stooped posture. She seems as fiery and feisty as that of a 20-year-old, and *I like it*.

CHAPTER FIVE

I've been working at the bookstore officially for eight days, and I'm absolutely in love with it. My duties mostly include invoicing, stocking, organizing, and sales. But the traffic is light, so it gives me plenty of time to grab a book off the shelf and read. It's peaceful in here, small enough that I can hear Bill and Caroline in the office when it's really quiet.

As I sit behind the desk on a thin four-legged stool, the door chimes, and I tilt my chin up from my book.

The sun is beaming in from the windows surrounding the front door, but what I see is something I can't really explain. A tall figure, a *familiar* tall figure, walks in. I rub my eye thoroughly, convinced I'm seeing things, but as this figure gets closer, my view becomes clearer.

"Vivian," he says with so much conviction my stomach drops. My heart instantly flutters at the sound of his voice. I almost forgot it, but when you hear it again, it's so distinctive, so unique. It's low and gruff, and when he says my name, the pit of my stomach knots.

"*Doctor*?" I question, almost angelic-like, with a grin plastered on my face unwillingly.

"How are you feeling? You look great," he says as he walks up to the counter, standing within arm's reach of me. "Well, I mean, not..hurt?" he continues as if he somehow put his foot in his mouth with the compliment.

"Thank you," I laugh.

His eyes brighten. "You work here?"

"Started a little over a week ago," I reply.

I can tell he is about to say something by the way his mouth parts but only a smile forms on his lips.

"Oh, Matthew!" Caroline shrills. "It's so nice to see you. Bill's in the back."

I must have a confused look on my face because Matt feels the need to explain to me what he's doing here.

"Bill and I play cards sometimes," he says, quickly shrugging his shoulders. His voice drops to a whisper as he playfully smiles. "He thinks he's the best at poker... he's not."

I laugh as he moves past me to the curtain, and I get a faint smell of him. Fresh, polished, and almost woodsy—like maybe his shampoo was some 'tough man hair care' kind of thing. No cologne, just clean. I catch a glimpse of the way his body moves now that he's so close to me. His bicep muscles are defined, even though he isn't flexing against the tighter short-sleeved shirt he has on. He's at least six feet tall, judging by my five-foot-four stature. His hair isn't styled, but the way it falls on top looks like he put some effort in. His scruff is still there, which happens to be one of my favorite parts about him.

"See you in a bit Viv," he says over his shoulder to me as he pushes through the curtain to the back.

Shit. My heart is fluttering again.

At least twenty minutes go by, and my shift is coming to an end. The boys are still in the back, and Caroline is dusting out front.

"You can clock out, sweetie." She calls from the corner of the store. I've been delaying clocking out, hoping Matt would leave soon and I would get to see him again.

"Ok, are you sure? I could stay a bit longer and take over dusting for you," I reply, hoping to squeeze out some extra time here.

"That's okay, Vivian. Go home and get some rest. You've been working so much your first week. We don't want to burn you out."

I don't want to continue pressing, so I agree and pack up my things. It sounds like Matt and Bill do this often, which gives me some hope I might see him again. I just wish I would have worn something better today. My white long-sleeve shirt only has three buttons in the center, which of course, are buttoned up, not exposing *any* cleavage.

It would have been nice to have some sort of heads-up. I would have ripped the buttons right off this fucking thing.

On my walk home from work, I call Lauren to let her know who visited the store today.

"Shut the hell up!" she screams on the other end. "Viv, are you kidding?" she continues.

"No, I'm dead serious," I say with a little laugh. "And before you ask, no, I didn't get his number, and I'm not going to ask for it either."

"You're such a chicken shit, ya know?" she says to me with a childlike voice.

"Get outta here!" I tease back. "I'll see you tomorrow Lo," I say as I hang up.

I'm not sure of the odds, and I don't know if I believe in destiny...but at this moment, I'm happy to see him again.

CHAPTER SIX

"Lox and bagels for me," I state to the waiter.

"Eggs and avocado toast, please," Lauren chimes in right after. "So what was he doing there again?" She shifts the direction of her gaze to me as the waiter leaves.

It's my day off, so Lauren and I decided to get brunch at our favorite spot downtown. I tried to make more of my appearance today since this restaurant is nearly across the street from the bookstore. If Matt visits there, he must be around this area or maybe live close by. I can't risk looking like shit if I might accidentally run into him again.

I put on my floral dress today. It's mid-length with slightly puffy sleeves and a lower neckline, exposing my décolletage along with the very tops of my breasts. My hair is curled loosely, almost reflecting beach waves, or at least, that's what I was going for.

"Playing cards with my boss?" I reply to her with a twisted smile.

"Interesting, and you...why do you look so..." she waves her straw in circles at me as if trying to come up with a word to describe me. "Nice," she finally gets out.

"Gee, thanks Lo," I laugh lightly. "I've got a job, I'm feeling great, and I wanted to actually get ready today," I say confidently, pleading my case that those are the *only* reasons.

Usually, when we come to brunch, I wear leggings and a zip-up with my sports bra underneath. I'm not generally one to dress to impress — I like to dress for comfort. Lauren, on the other hand, dresses to impress even when she's going to bed. I knew she'd take notice of me wearing something nice, at brunch, no less. The sight of my hair being done probably is what shocked her the most.

"Well, you look great, Viv," she says with her full lips pressed together in a smile. "So, how does the hot doc know your boss?" She takes a drink of her water as her eyebrows perk up.

"I have no clue. I haven't had a chance to ask. My shift was over before they were done, and I didn't want to ask Caroline." *Even though I really did.* "But it seems like they do it often. The way they all greeted each other was like they have all been friends for years."

"When do you work next?"

"Not until Monday. I'm off the whole weekend," I say with a smile.

"Let's go out before I leave!"

As our food comes out, we continue to talk and catch up. She keeps telling me all of the 'signs' that she's getting proposed to on vacation. I keep dismissing them, telling her that's just a coincidence.

"I think you're overthinking it," I say. I have to keep a straight face to avoid ruining her surprise. She's been waiting for this since the day they first met. When she came back to my house after their first date, she said, *I'm going to marry that man one day*, and the rest is history. I wish I could be there for that moment, but Carter told me he hired a videographer, so I'll get to see it at least.

We finish our brunch and go shopping for something to wear this weekend. It's not that I don't already have clothes. I just want to find something a little more risqué than things I already own.

After the accident, I thought a lot about my life. Had I died that night, I would have died a sad and lonely 24-year-old. Hardly any friends, no family, and not even enough people in my life to carry my casket. How fucked up is that? I don't want my life to continue this way. I have to put myself out there more. I have to meet new people and crawl out of the comfortable shell I've been living in. I need to start dating and stop with casual sex, even though the thought of it makes me sick.

At the store, I find a slinky black mini dress that seems to be Lo's favorite pick, even though the way it hugs my body makes me a little uncomfortable. The neckline is somewhat of a sweetheart but holds my breasts up without a bra, nice and high.

"Perfect," I say, coming out of the dressing room to see Lauren.

"Holy tits!" she exclaims with wide eyes.

"Ya like?" I say as I do a slight twirl around.

"I do, I do." Lauren pulls at the slit on my dress. "I'll buy. My treat."

"You're not going to buy my fucking dress, Lauren," I command back at her.

She gives me a snarky smile in reply. "Yes, I am, *Vivian*, and watch your mouth, or I'm going to buy you new shoes too."

"You don't have to do that, Lo..." I say to her with a modest voice.

"I know, but I want to. I'm proud of you for getting a job so quickly, and I'm happy you love it. I just want to see you do great things. Save your paycheck, this ones on me."

I don't like it when she does this, pays for me. Sometimes she'll pay for my brunch, and I feel terrible that I can't reciprocate for her. Usually, I just have enough to buy my own, but she knows that.

We get up to the counter to checkout after she convinced me to get thin-strapped black heels to match. They are about as slinky as this dress is.

What I find fascinating is how such little material could be so expensive. Shouldn't it be cheaper since the material is about enough to only swaddle a newborn? I tell Lauren I feel bad about the price, but she still insists it's on her. She tells me the way it hugs my curves should be a sin.

Whatever that means.

I don't argue with her; I just let her pay. That's another one hundred and fifty dollars to add to my tab to her for when I get rich.

CHAPTER SEVEN

"U ber will be here in five," I tell Lauren as I look at the app on my phone.

"You look great, Viv," she says while looking at me through the mirror.

I smile at her and take a step back to observe our outfits of the night. Lauren is wearing sequins, high-waisted pants, and a black slinky bralette to match. Her bright blonde hair is down and full of life with the rollers she used to dry it. Her skin is fair but still glowing as if it's porcelain, and her dark red lipstick lines her lips that are full from the filler she got two weeks ago.

I have the dress she bought me, only it presses tightly over my chest as if I should have bought a bigger size, but having done so- it wouldn't hug my hips as tight as it does. I like how the dress makes it seem like my figure is an hourglass, even though I don't really think it is. My hair is polished and smooth, thanks to my weekly conditioning treatments, and it falls a little above the middle of my back when it is completely straight. I style my bangs the same way I always do, so they frame my face like curtains and line my lips with a darker liner — only adding lip gloss. I'm not bold enough to try a color like Lauren always does.

As we head for the door to wait for our ride outside, I grab my small silver clutch and throw my keys in. I'm getting more and more anxious as the time on my app clocks down for when the car will arrive. I haven't been in one since Lauren drove me home from the hospital, and even then, I closed my eyes the entire time.

To say I'm feeling sick is an *understatement.*

My phone chimes that our driver is here, and Lauren and I bustle out of my house. As I lock up, she hops in the car and scoots over to the other side, and I make my way to the car door and pause just enough for me to get a deep sigh out.

"We're going to be okay," Lauren says as she pats the seat next to her as if for me to sit.

While we are driving, I try to keep my eyes shut. At every quick break or weaving of traffic, I close my eyes even tighter. Whenever Lauren notices, she just squeezes my left hand for reassurance.

Had I known this route would take us past that same intersection of my crash, I probably would have told her we needed to choose a different club.

"Be careful!" I shout to the driver involuntarily as we come up on the light as if this isn't what this man does for a living.

He glares at me through the rear-view mirror but continues. As we are passing through, I drop my head into the seat to make sure I can't see and clench my stomach for some sense of security.

"All through," Lauren says softly as we continue on easily.

The car ride is at least fifteen minutes to get us into the city, and I *maybe* have looked out the window twice, and both times were accidental.

"Have a good night, ladies," the driver says to us as we exit his Toyota.

Stepping out at the curb, I feel like I can finally breathe, as if this dress wasn't tight enough, I feel like I'm suffocating after that ride.

"You good?" Lauren says as she laces her arm into mine, guiding me to the front door.

"Yeah, I'm good. That was rough. Don't you think he was going a little fast?"

"He was going the speed limit, Viv, I checked. It's okay, we're here now." Her voice is calm, never changing or rising, and I appreciate it. I know I sound frantic, but I can't help it.

"I don't know about you, but I'm ready for a drink. I'm going to try to not remember the ride home," I say with a laugh, even though I'm absolutely serious.

"I want whatever white wine you have, and she'll take..." Lauren says to the bartender.

"I'll take a vodka soda with two limes," I order, only taking a second to pause before I add, "Make it a double."

The lighting in here is dark, followed by colored lights that sometimes sweep the crowd. The club is pretty large, and tonight it's packed. The music they are playing is *okay*, not typically my favorite. Mostly remixes of songs I like, with more bass and techno sounds.

Lauren and I stand at the bar, hoping one of the patrons sitting will get up soon to dance so we can take their seats. The bar is one of the longest I've seen, and somehow every stool is occupied.

"It's busy tonight," I shout to Lauren.

"Isn't that April?" She shouts back.

April was in our accounting class with us. She's nice enough. Kind of mousy, with a shrill voice. It's quite annoying at times, but she means well.

"Hey, April!" I yell so she can hear me over the music.

She spotted us first and was already making her way over. As she comes up, two gentlemen sitting near us get up, and Lauren and I immediately replace their spots.

"How are you girls? I haven't seen you in so long. How's Carter?" April asks us.

"Carter is good," Lauren responds. "We're all good, just busy!"

"How's your mom and dad?" I ask April.

In college, April's parents used to send the best care packages to her. Since Lauren's dorm was across the hall from hers, we would regularly get to snack on whatever goodies they brought. These care packages were huge and filled with anything you could imagine. Face masks, Pringles, Diet Coke, gift cards to restaurants nearby, laundry detergent, you name it, they bought it. I remember thinking her parents must be rich by how much they were dropping on these care packages. It did make me a little envious at times, only because by the time I was in college, my parents were not around.

"They are good! They just got back from Lake Tahoe. My dad said he was thinking about buying a house there," she replies in her squeaky voice.

As we continue talking about April's rich parents, I notice a man staring in our direction, although he's probably just looking at Lauren. I keep sipping on my drink, casually glancing over at him only to catch him looking back at us. He's cute — *enough.* His hair is short, almost buzzed, and his strong jaw seems square with how it takes shape. He's taller than most of the men he's standing with, and he must be funny, too, because every time I look over, he's making his friends laugh.

April sees some other acquaintances, so she excuses herself from our area. Lauren and I swing our legs a bit to the front of our chairs and look at each other.

"Still annoying as ever," Lauren laughs.

"She's not *that* bad," I say back to her with a bigger laugh.

"Lauren, look... is that guy staring at you or me?" I slyly point in his direction.

I wasn't sly enough because he starts to make his way over, weaving in and out of the crowd until he gets right behind us.

"Can I buy you a drink?" the man says, looking directly into my eyes.

"Me?" I shrill back, confused because I for sure thought he was after Lauren.

"Yes, you," he says with a smile.

His smile is nice. Nowhere nearly as beautiful as 'Matt the Doctor', though.

"Sure," I reply, feeling Lauren nudge my leg under the lip of the bar.

"I have to go to the bathroom. I'll be right back," Lauren says as she leans into me.

I know that bitch doesn't have to use the bathroom, and if she did, she would make me go with her. I think she has bathroom anxiety — she can't go alone in public restrooms and always needs company. I'm surprised she's walking away on her own.

"Mind if I sit," the man says. His voice is gentle but thick at the same time.

"Not at all. Go right ahead. But I warn you, I might kick you out of the seat when she comes back." I giggle.

"My name is Sebastian. What's yours?"

"Vivian," I say. "But you can call me Viv."

"Nice to meet you, Viv. Are you from around here?"

"I live close," I say, only trying not to divulge the exact location. I watch enough true crime to know exactly what happens when you tell the wrong person the right information.

He continues to ask me questions about myself, acting genuinely interested in everything I have to say. It's refreshing, and I appreciate it.

It's been at least a couple of minutes by now, and Lauren still isn't back, but the next drink I ordered for her is waiting at the bar in front of Sebastian. I'm already halfway finished with mine because talking to random people peeks my anxiety, and with a drink in my hand, it's much easier to tolerate.

"You want another?" He says. "It's on me."

You're damn right it is.

"Sure," I say with a sweet smile.

Lauren finally returns after what seems like ages, and Sebastian quickly stands up from the seat, pulling it out for her. He introduces himself to her, and we all make conversation lightly. He asks us what we do for a living, and we ask him back. He tells us he manages a bank just outside of the city, but he doesn't seem like the *I work at a bank* type. He seems more like he rides motorcycles and wears leather jackets to *bed* type. Maybe it's the silver rings he has on his hands or the tattoos I see peeking out from the ends of his long sleeve. Whatever it is, it just doesn't scream bank to me. It's more...*bad boy*.

Sebastian moves to stand closer to my seat, resting his hand on the back of my chair. He offers to buy me another drink, but I'm not even finished with the last one he got. He insists he'll pay for the next one when I'm ready and asks me to dance instead.

I hate dancing, but this dress is so tight with me sitting down — I really should stand soon, or else my body is going to go numb from the loss of blood in my torso. I eventually agree and bring my drink to the dance floor. I begged Lauren to join, but she said she's going to hold the fort down and save our seats.

Three drinks in are serving me well. I haven't drunk this much since before my accident, and my tolerance must have shifted because I have a pretty strong buzz going.

Sebastian takes my hand and spins me, so my back is pressed to his chest. It's a rap song playing, and everyone is grinding on the dance floor. I'm guessing those are the only moves you can do with this type of song.

He lowers his hand to my hip and pushes himself into me until I can feel his belt on my lower back. His head lowers to the dip of my neck as we move with the music, and I close my eyes as I grind on him, enjoying every second of the attention. I turn my head to look at him only for a moment before his arm stretches across my lower belly, securing me tighter onto him.

"You're really beautiful, Vivian," he says, only loud enough to faintly hear over the music.

I roll my hips with the music as he grips me tighter. My dress keeps rising as I move, so I have to adjust frequently. It's already too short, and the last thing I want to do is give this whole club a free peek.

"Let me get you another," Sebastian says while touching my empty glass. I oblige because I'm already feeling fantastic. My goal was to not remember the ride home, and that's exactly what I intended to do. I walk back to the bar with him to check on Lauren, only to see her bobbing her head to the music with a grin.

"You all good?" I ask her.

"Absolutely," she replies. "You having fun out there?"

"Yeah, but I don't want to leave you alone! I'm going to stay here with you for a bit."

"No, no, go ahead and get back out there. I have a headache coming on. I was going to see if you wouldn't mind having Carter come pick me up. We can come back and get you, though, so you don't have to ride home alone!" she says.

"That's fine, Lo! Go ahead and don't worry about getting me. I feel great. I'll be fine riding by myself," I say with slurred words.

As Sebastian hands me my next drink, we continue talking with Lauren until Carter arrives.

"Want to get back out there?" Sebastian asks me as soon as she's gone.

I don't reply. Instead, I just offer him my hand to take me back to the dance floor.

We resume our position with my back pressed firmly against the front of him. We move in a slow grind, and he places his hand on my upper thigh. I reach my hand around the back of his neck, only to bring his head closer to my neck, and I close my eyes as we move to the song.

Sebastian grips my thigh tighter, causing me to wince out in pain, quiet enough for him not to hear beneath the pumping base of the song. His rings pinch my skin as he grips, and the feeling is less than desirable. I move his hand away from my upper thigh, but he quickly places it back, this time trying to inch his hand up even further under my dress.

He grips the hand on my hip harder, and whatever he's doing now is too rough for me on the dance floor, so I spin around and lie to him, telling him I need to go to the restroom. He shoots a confused look at me, but I don't give it a second thought before I leave the dance floor and head for the restrooms.

I barge in and walk straight to the mirror, placing my hands on the sink. I feel hot and annoyed I was just man-handled. I look down and see my skin reacting to his touch. My thigh is imprinted with red marks in the shape of his fingers, and I scoff as my eyes roll to the back of my head. I look up at myself in the mirror and can tell my eyes are heavy, I'm visibly intoxicated at this point, and it's time for me to go home.

"Sober up," I drunkenly demand to myself in the mirror.

I splash some cold water on my neck and shoulders to cool myself off before I head out of the bathroom. As soon as I swing the door open, Sebastian's eyes lock with mine.

"There you are," he says as he grips my elbows. My hands are in daggers, separating my chest from his. I try to release his grip, but he just holds me tighter. "Let's get out of here," he whispers as his hot breath touches the crook in my neck. This time, I can smell the liquor on his breath. He had been getting Old Fashions at the bar and had as many as I did, not counting any he had before he came over to Lauren and me.

"I should be getting home," I say to him, trying not to sound timid.

"Let me take you." His face is still close to mine. I'm trying to move away, but the drinks I had are affecting my strength to get out of his grip.

"No, thank you, my friends should be in the parking lot right now waiting for me," I lie between my teeth.

"Come on, Viv, let me take you home." He releases his grip on my elbow, tugging on the thin strap of my dress.

"No, it's really fine, thank you," I say, trying to unclench his fingers from the material.

His face presses close to mine. "Viv, I want to see what's under this dress."

"I need to go now," I say, trying to back up, but his grip moves to the small of my back, locking me in. "I need to leave, Sebastian."

"I promise I can make you feel good." He says, tugging on my strap so hard that it finally breaks.

It was thin to begin with, but his tugging just released the threads holding it together. I quickly bring my hand up, stopping the dress from falling and uncovering my left breast.

"She said no!" A voice yells nearby. Not giving me enough time to turn my head to see who it is before Sebastian is shoved into a wall.

I back up hastily to make room for what looks to be a fight, and I see the man towering over Sebastian, gripping his shirt by the collar.

"Get the fuck out of here," the man shouts. I'm trying to place his voice, but my head is pounding to the beat of the music. My last drink must have caught up quickly with all this commotion going on, and it's hard for me to keep a steady focus.

As the man shoves Sebastian, he turns towards me, and that's when I see him. The scruff, the tousled hair, the blazing eyes.

"Matt! What are you doing here?" I say with a heavy breath, still holding the top of my left breast so my dress doesn't fall.

He doesn't respond right away. He just continues to walk towards me, taking his jacket off and sweeping it across my shoulders.

"Put this on, and I'll take you home," he says in his low voice.

I don't get a chance to respond as he grabs my shoulders and tucks me into him, guiding me out the door.

"I - I didn't pay my tab yet," I stammer.

"I'll call the club and pay it later. I'm parked just around the corner. Is it okay if I take you home?" He asks as we get outside.

"Yes," I say. My eyelids become heavier by the second, and my body sways accidentally.

Once we reach his car, he opens the car door and ushers for me to sit. I look up, realizing I'm seeing double but still mentally aware I'm in a car, and not just anyone's car — *Matthews's* car.

The one I hit.

As he gets in, he pauses and shifts his body toward me.

"Are you okay?" He says with a softened gaze.

"I'm fine," I say. "Thank you..." I trail off as I notice him looking at my thigh. The red handprint mark is still visible, and even more noticeable that I'm sitting and my dress has shortened significantly more than it already was.

His eyes darken with what I could imagine is rage. His cupid's bow is pressed in almost a thin tight line. He looks upset, and I'm not sure if it's with me or the situation of it all.

He shifts himself in his seat and starts the car. After he pings in the address I gave him into his GPS, he places his right arm on the back of my seat and looks over his shoulder to back out. The light tan shirt tucked into the black pants he has on fits him loosely. His skin, in this lighting, looks tan against the silver watch on his wrist, and the veins in his forearms protrude as he drives. To me, he's never looked sexier.

"What are you doing by yourself?" He asks as if I'm incapable of handling my own.

"I was with Lauren. She left," I say flatly.

I usually don't get car sick, but this ride is making me extremely dizzy. I feel almost groggy. I try to direct my attention back to Matt so I can regain focus, but there are two of him right now, and I'm not sure which one is the real Matt to focus on. It's as if this car ride somehow made me ten times more intoxicated.

"Are you feeling okay?" I hear Matthew ask, but it's hard for me to regain control over my head to turn and look at him.

Suddenly I feel almost paralyzed like my body is too weak to make any movements. I've never felt like this after drinking before, so I fear something is wrong.

"I think I," I manage to muster before my jaw stiffens, and I close my eyes.

That fuck Sebastian, I think he roofied me.

CHAPTER EIGHT

The sun is beaming through the windows by my front door as I peel open my eyes, realizing they are entirely way too sensitive to the light.

What in the hell happened?

I sit up slowly and rub my eyes, feeling like complete shit. I look around my living room, confused as to why I wasn't in bed. I see a disheveled blanket and a pillow on the other side of my sectional and look down at myself to see I'm wearing my dad's old Chicago Bears t-shirt, *backward*, with no pants on. As I'm trying to piece memories of last night together, the toilet flushes in the bathroom off of my kitchen, and I snap my head around to see who else is in my house with me.

"Oh shit, you scared me," Matt says with a little laugh. "I didn't know you were up."

I stare in awe at him as I'm still trying to piece things together.

"You stayed here?" I ask him, genuinely confused.

"I'm sorry. You were so sick...I didn't want to leave you."

"Sick?" I ask.

"Yeah, in the car, you were pretty drunk. I brought you up the stairs to your door, and you threw up all down the front of your dress. I brought you in and stuck you in the shower while I washed off your front porch with some water and a cup I found on the counter."

Oh my god. I did what? I can't even respond. I'm mortified about the conversation we're having right now.

"I hope you don't mind. I found a t-shirt on your floor and just threw it on you after I got you out of the shower," he says.

"You dressed me?"

"Well, yeah. I couldn't let you stay in the vomit dress, and I wanted to be respectful and not leave you naked either."

"*Naked?*"

"Yes, Vivian, but I didn't look at anything I shouldn't. Don't worry. I just wanted to help. I tried calling your friend Lauren, but your phone was already dead, and I didn't save her number from when I called her after the accident," he states with a sorrowed look.

"Matt," I stop him. "It's okay. Thank you. I'm really sorry. I think I got roofied. I usually can handle my liquor, but as soon as I got in the car, things really went south, and honestly, I have no recollection of any of this."

"Jesus," he says, putting his hand on his forehead in disbelief. "Should I- do we need to- " he asks before I cut him off.

"I'm fine now. I have a raging headache, and my mouth tastes disgusting, but I'm fine. Thank you for staying."

"Do you want to call the police?" he asks as he moves closer to me, placing his hands on the back of my couch.

"No- it's done. I'm fine."

"I'll fucking kill him," Matt snaps after some silence, his eyebrows burrowing and his lips pressed thin.

"Matt, *it's fine.* It's done with," I tell him, lifting my hand to calm him.

"Do you need anything?"

"Can you hand me the Tylenol? It's in the cupboard on the right next to the sink." My head is pounding, and the light peering in is still bothering my sight.

"Can you also shut the blinds?" I ask as I point toward my front door.

Matt shuts the blinds, brings me a cup of water with two Tylenol, and then sits on the other sectional.

"You really didn't have to stay," I say to him, looking up from my water glass.

"I couldn't just leave you, Viv," he says with softened eyes.

I put my head down and soak in his words. His voice is soothing. The way he speaks sends fire to the pit of my stomach, warming me like a cashmere blanket. A blanket I never want to get out from under.

"What were you at the club for?" I ask with a soft voice.

"It was a buddy of mine's birthday. They all wanted to go there after we ate dinner."

"Why did you almost fight that guy?" I ask another question.

"I saw you with him. I thought you guys knew each other at first the way you were dancing. When I saw him follow you to the bathroom, I moved closer to where you were, just in case. Then I saw him grab you. I thought he was handling you a little rough, so I kept my eyes on you. When I heard you kept saying you needed to leave and realized he wasn't letting you go, that's when I figured you didn't know him. And when I saw him rip your dress and I, I fucking lost it. I'm really sorry."

"You don't have to be sorry," I quietly say. "I just met him, and everything was fine until he started grabbing me too hard. But you left your friends. You didn't have to do that. You could have stayed and drank with them."

"I wanted to leave, and I don't really drink anymore. I would have rather you gotten home safe anyways."

"So you were watching me the whole night?" I blurt out.

"Well, when you put it like that, it sounds stalker-ish." He laughs nervously. "I saw you come in with your friend. I noticed you right away. I didn't want to bother you. I figured you were having a 'girls' night'. So I just let you be."

I press my lips together and tilt my head down, looking at the water glass in my hands.

"How old are you?" I ask as I look up. This is the most I have gotten to talk to him, and I feel like I want to know anything and everything there is to know. After all, he is in *my* house. I should have a right to know.

"Twenty-seven." He smiles.

I grin back with closed lips and proceed to my next question.

"Why do you play cards with Bill?"

Matthew gives a little laugh, then says, "I was a little shit growing up. My brother and I grew up in foster care and never had a steady home. By the time I turned fourteen, I was drinking and just causing terror everywhere." He continues, "And now..don't hate me or anything... but I did some messed up shit when I was younger, but I promise I'm nothing like that anymore." He smirks.

I look at him with a soft stare soaking in his words. "I put dog shit in a bag and lit it on fire. I set it on a porch and rang the doorbell."

"Matthew!" I yell jokingly.

"Well…" He grins. "The house was Mr. and Mrs. Birch's, and apparently, I didn't run fast enough because Bill caught me. Long story short, I owe them everything. Bill and Caroline pushed me to do better in life. I don't think I would be where I am today without them. Most of Bill's friends have passed, and that man loves to play cards. Anytime I get a free moment, I make it a point to visit and play poker with him."

"They really are wonderful people," I add.

"I agree," he says.

"I like working for them."

"From what I could tell, they're enjoying you too."

There's a pause, where we both sit in silence. I'm thinking about the million more things I want to ask him, but he quickly breaks the quiet.

"Listen, I have to go home and sleep a little bit before my shift. Is there somewhere I can leave my number in case you need anything?"

"You didn't get enough sleep?" I ask curiously.

"I didn't want you to get sick in the middle of the night, so I kept waking up to check on you. I tried to turn you on your side, but you kept fighting me to lay on your back, so I just gave up." He chuckles, which makes me blush.

Getting blackout drunk and waking up to hear about all the embarrassing things you did the night before is one thing. It's another thing to have the sexiest man you've ever seen in your *life* be the one to tell you about all of the embarrassing things you did the night before.

I stand up to find a piece of paper he can write his number on because I'm absolutely not going to pass up the opportunity to get it.

As I start to stand, I realize my balance is still thrown off, and I quickly become light-headed. Matt sees this and almost immediately stands up to grab my arm to balance me.

"I think I need to eat," I say — mostly to myself.

"Do you have something here? I can run out and grab you something if you'd like," he says as he walks me to the kitchen.

"I can find something, go home and get some sleep," I mumble as I grab an old envelope that once had my electric bill in it. Grabbing a pen, I hand them both to him.

"When your phone is turned on, text me so I can save your number, please."

"Yes, sir." I smirk. I think the alcohol is still in my system. I didn't mean for it to sound so sensual.

Matthew grins and gives me the envelope back. My fingers brush against his as I take it from him. His fingers are warm, and the sensation feels like ice against my cold hands.

"I'm serious. Let me know if you need anything today," he says once he places a hand on my doorknob.

I give him a thumbs-up and a smile. As he opens the door to walk out, I yell one last, "Thank you!"

He nods with a pressed grin, only a slight dimple showing on the side of his mouth, and then he shuts my door behind him.

CHAPTER NINE

"Ho-Ly *SHIT!*" Lauren yells. "I should have never left you alone, Viv. What the fuck was I thinking? He *pushed* him? *And* stayed the night at your house?" Lauren is going a mile a minute.

After my phone turned on, I had twelve text messages from her asking where I was, if I was okay, who I was with...you know, the usual *mom* texts. I called her and told her to meet me at D'Maggios, our favorite brunch spot, since I so desperately needed to eat. I spilled the entire night to her, or what I could remember, plus what Matthew had told me.

"And you haven't texted him yet? Text him now. What the fuck are you doing, Viv?" she says with a wide-eyed grin.

"Okay, Okay, relax. I'm still trying to sober up." I laugh.

"I can't believe you got drugged. I should have never left you. I'm so sorry, Vivian. I will never do that again. I was so happy you seemed to be having a good time and wanted you to get some action. Not, ya know, getting drugged action but..." she stops as the waiter gets our drinks.

"It's fine, Lo. I promise Matt was there."

"And what if he hadn't been Vivian?" Her eyes drop in a way that makes me think she's going to spend the next few weeks beating herself up over this.

"Then I would be dead in a ditch somewhere," I say, smiling, shrugging my shoulders, only trying to lighten the mood. I know the situation could have been a lot worse. *But it wasn't.*

"No need to dwell on things that didn't happen."

She runs her fingers through her hair. "I'm sorry again."

"Lauren, stop. I'm a big girl. There's going to be situations in my life you can't Mom me through or get me out of."

Her eyebrows arch. "That sounds like a challenge."

The waiter brings our mimosas as I open my phone to text Matthew.

Me: Hi, it's Vivian. I'm all good. Thank you again for last night. I owe you one.

I can't even begin to try and be flirty with this text because the man saw me puke on myself. There's nothing sexy about that.

I start to ask Lauren what she has planned for the day, but just as I open my mouth, my phone dings.

Matthew: Did you eat?

Me: I'm at a restaurant with Lauren right now.

Matthew: Okay. Do you have any muscle pain?

Me: Um...I don't think so? Should I?

Matthew: It's common after getting roofied to still have side effects. Muscle pain can be one of them.

Me: Oh, okay. Thank you, Doctor.

I close my phone with a grin.

"Matt?" Lauren asks.

"Matt." I bite my bottom lip with a smile.

Lauren and I order our food and continue talking about all her preparations for the Hamptons with Carter. I convince her we should get our nails done today and just blame it on the possibility I may see Matt again. I don't give a shit about my nails. I hardly ever have them done. But I know Lauren—and she would be *furious* if I knew she was about to get proposed to, and I let her do so with neglected fingernails and dry cuticles. We finish eating and head to the nail salon, where she insists on a bright color. Thankfully, I convince her otherwise and have her go with a simple french manicure.

I take the long route home to walk once we're finished. I want to stop by the liquor store and grab a bottle of wine. My hangover is raging, and if I learned anything from college, it's that the cure right now for me is the *hair of the dog*.

It's a nice day out, so I don't mind walking the extra four blocks, and a little exercise today won't hurt. I've got nowhere to be tonight, so my idea of a good time is some wine and that new movie on Netflix I've been dying to see.

I round the corner and can see my house. I say house, but it's more of a townhome — one set of stairs leads up to my front door, and a separate set of stairs leads down to the neighbor's kid's apartment. There also is another door right next to mine with a tiny bit of space in between with the same setup on the opposite side. Our large building is split between four homes, and the burnt red brick contrasts with the dark black doors.

When I first moved in, they gave me a hell of a deal on the rent since I was in college. I convinced them to keep my rent the same if I paid them well in advance. I'm not an idiot, the way renting prices are — I got a fucking steal.

I love my home. I really don't have any intentions of ever leaving. I mean, unless they sell the place.

Making my way to the door, I see the neighbor boys on their stairs.

"Did you frow up?" the smallest boy asks while pointing to my stoop. I look closer to see some leftover residue Matt didn't manage to wash away.

"I think it was a dog," I say, shrugging my shoulders, knowing damn well that was, in fact, me.

"That's gwoss!" he says.

"I agree, little man," I say with a slight smile

I get inside and plop my brown paper bag on the island in my kitchen. Whipping out my phone, I decide to order sushi. What a perfect night. Wine, Sushi, Movies. Could this get any better? Laying underneath Matt as he thrusts into me could make it a hell of a lot better, but for all I know, this man has a wife I don't know about. Unfortunately, when he was having a sleepover with me, I failed to ask him about that key factor.

I'm already starting to feel a little buzz after two glasses of wine and forty minutes into this movie. That really wasn't the goal with drinking tonight, but I have to admit that this buzz feels better on my head than my brain swelling from the hangover.

My doorbell rings, and I spring up to answer, touching my cheeks to feel their warmth from the red wine. Sushi is here, and now it's *really* a party. There's something about sashimi and a dragon roll that really brings joy to my life.

As I divulge in my favorite foods, I hear a ping from my phone in the kitchen.

Matthew: Did I leave my jacket there?

I glance around my kitchen and peer into the living room from the large arched opening in the wall that separates the two. From this view, I can only see my two sectional pieces, my fireplace with the TV hanging above and the left window next to my door. I step into the living room to view the other side when I see his black jacket hanging over the banister to my stairs.

Me: yess it's here I can brisng it to the bookstore and leave it behind the counter if yoiu want
Matthew: Are you drunk?
Me: not relly
Matthew: Where are you?
Me: home.

I'm really 0 for 3 with this guy. The first time we met, I rammed my car into his and was covered in blood. The second time I puked on myself. This time, I'm drunk texting him. He probably thinks I'm an alcoholic erratic driver.

Wonderful.

I spend the remainder of my night eating the rest of my sushi, finishing my movie, and tucking myself into bed. I set an alarm for eight in the morning, so I can get in a quick run before work. *Assuming I won't wake up with another hangover.*

Sliding into my sheets and wrapping myself under my covers, I relax, listening to the sounds of cars passing by, their occasional honks, and the wind.

This. Is. *Bliss.*

CHAPTER TEN

The bell rings above the front door to Birch Books as I walk in, and Caroline lifts her head from the computer to see me.

"Hello dear!" she says with a cheeky grin.

"Good afternoon! Has it been busy today?" I ask as I move towards the front desk with Matthew's jacket draped over my arms.

"It's been steady," she says, which usually means it's been slow. The only time I've ever known this place to fill up is if we get an author in town who does a book signing here. It's okay, though. I like the 'steady' business that comes through. It's quaint and peaceful. And the entire vibe of the store would be thrown off if it was jam-packed every day.

I set Matthew's jacket underneath the opening behind the counter and stand up straight to adjust my jeans, I usually don't wear high-waisted pants, but I liked how these straight-legged mom jeans fit around my ass. They hug perfectly around the curve of my lower back.

I'm restocking books and organizing titles about two hours into my shift when I hear the bell above the front door chime. As I'm holding four books at a time, I swing my body around to face the front door. The light from the window is casting on me as I see him walk in.

"Hi, Matt," I say with an unexpected smile. "Are you here to see Bill?"

"No, I actually was..." he says while taking two steps toward me. "Well, I wanted to see if you were free later tonight?"

"Me?" I ask while snapping my head back.

I think I'm in disbelief at this point. I'm just shocked that after this weekend, the man of my *literal dreams* still wants to take me out.

"Yes." He laughs. "You." I set the books down on a table nearby and take a step towards him as I raise my hand up to take the claw-clip out of my hair. As it is released, I shake out the tresses that were pinned, letting them unravel and fall to the mid of my back as my arm drops to my side.

"What would you like to do?" I grin.

"There is a new restaurant downtown I've been meaning to try, and I wanted to see if you would like to go with me."

"What time?" I say as I slide my hands into my back pockets.

"Mmm, seven o'clock?" he states like a question to which he already knows the answer.

"Can we walk there?"

"Do you not want to drive?"

"Not really."

"Well, it'd be a hell of a walk," he says with a laugh and slight nod.

"We can drive," I say with a deep breath.

I'll be fine. I'll just...shut my eyes nonchalantly.

"Oh! I have your jacket, I exclaim, walking towards the counter. "Listen, I'm really sorry about the other night."

"The drunk text?"

"Okay, well...I'm sorry for last night and the night before," I say, embarrassed.

"It's really okay, Vivian. It's nothing to apologize for," he says with a soft smile. His eyes seem more golden in the store lighting, and I can't help but do anything except completely melt looking at him.

"Okay, I'll see you tonight. Do you remember where I live?"

"I think I'll manage," he says, nodding his head *yes* with a smile before he starts to walk out.

I catch him just in time to yell, "I forgot, one last thing!" *he stops to turn and look at me.* "You're not married, are you?" I say with a light laugh to try to mask my seriousness.

"No," he says with a smile dropping his eyes down the length of my body. "Not even close." His eyes make their way back to mine before he turns to leave.

Oh, my stomach is dropping. That fucking grin of his. Every time he smiles, it runs over my body like hot liquid.

As I finish my shift, I go back to tell Bill and Caroline goodbye. I see Caroline sitting in the chair on the opposite side of Bill, leaning back as he reads a book to her with his elbows on the desk.

"Goodbye, Vivian," Bill says with a raspy voice and a grin.

"Bye, Vivy! We'll see ya tomorrow," Caroline says with a little twang.

I don't know what it is with those two. I could sit and talk with them for hours. Bill always has some kind of life quote he likes to spew out too. Some of his favorites are *Be Proud of Your Progress* and *Above All, Try*— If angels walk this earth, it's Bill and Caroline.

I head home to get ready for Matt to pick me up. The thought of that alone sends icy chills running down my spine, and I remember I haven't talked to Lo since she told me they arrived at the house they're staying in. I quickly send her a text before I walk in the door to let her know who asked me out. I'm sure she will be thrilled to hear.

I keep my high-waisted jeans on and change into heels before I head to my bathroom and fix my hair, still keeping it in the claw clip it was earlier. I look at my reflection and trace the scar on my head. It runs from my middle part down to the top of my ear, a little out from my hairline. I fix my hair back in place and add lip gloss, curling my eyelashes before I head back downstairs.

I grab my phone off of the table and throw it in a small black purse I picked from my closet, and just as I head to my kitchen to grab some water, my doorbell rings.

I spin around, drop my purse on the kitchen island, and head for the door.

Matt! You're early," I say, somewhat *too* excited.

"I was counting on a lot more traffic tonight," he replies, looking slightly embarrassed.

He changed the shirt he wore when he entered the store this afternoon. He's wearing a gray loose-fitting t-shirt with small white writing in the center and dark blue jeans. Standing in front of me with his left hand in his pocket, I can see the veins in his strong hands and, for a moment, wonder what it would feel like if he put that same hand to use on me.

"Come in," I say with a closed mouth smile. "I just have to grab my purse, and we can get going."

He follows me inside, and deep down, I hope he's staring at my ass. This is the moment I'm thankful that I kept these jeans on.

Looking at Matthew in my house sends flooding waves over my body. It's hard for me to stop myself from ripping my clothes off and jumping on him right here. The way he looks, how he walks, how he talks, everything he does sends shivers down to my core.

I have to take it slow with him.

I *need* to take it slow with him.

I think that's why my past dating life has been so un-successful. We get intimate too soon, and the heat and excitement are lost, or I find out they're a lousy lover and never call them again. I want nothing more than to fuck Matt on the kitchen floor that he's standing on, but I've got to contain myself if there's any hope of keeping him around. I know myself, and as much as I want him, I need to relax.

"How long have you lived here?" He asks while placing his hands on my kitchen island.

"A little over six years," I say to him.

"Are you from Boston?"

"I grew up in Chicago. What about you?"

"Born and raised here." He says with a grin.

I divulge a little of what it was like growing up in Chicago as we walk out the door. I tell him what my favorite place to eat around there was and that I could walk to Wrigley field from our first home. I also tell him how my family and I would visit Michigan sometime in the summer.

As we get to his car, my nerves are already starting to work up. I look around and can't find a single scratch on it. I know he probably got it fixed right away, but it makes me sad that the first car I purchased was completely totaled.

He opens the passenger door for me, and I get in. Taking a deep breath as he rounds the front to get in on his side.

"You ready?" He glances at me with a closed smile while pushing the button to start his car. I nod. Even though I want to shake my head *no*.

Him driving is fine. I think I'm doing an *okay* job at closing my eyes. Occasionally I will glance over at him, so he assumes I'm 'looking around'. When I'm ready to close my eyes again, I just pretend to stare out my window. It's actually working out flawlessly for me. Until, of course, we get to that damned intersection. I figured it was coming. Not many decent restaurants are the opposite way. This one, though, is harder to fake. I try what I can to prepare for it, but as we get closer, it just doesn't feel right. I shut my eyes tight and drop my head to hide my sight from the windows. Matthew must have noticed because right as we are about to go through, he grabs my left hand and squeezes. Once he lets go, I figure that's the signal we are finished, so I reluctantly open my eyes.

"Do you have trouble in cars?" he asks, slightly glancing at me.

I don't respond. I just shrug my shoulders and curl the ends of my lips in whatever smile I can form at the moment. I don't know what I could say to him other than I'm deathly afraid to be in this vehicle right now. I'm not worried about him driving. I'm worried about everyone else.

We finally arrive after what seemed like eighty hours but in reality was probably twenty-five minutes. After he's parked the car, he opens my door, lending me a hand to hold on to while I get out.

The restaurant is *cute*. At each table outside is a closed umbrella in the middle. The string lights hanging off the awning make it look like stars glistening in the nighttime, and there is a thin black gate enclosing the outside seating area. As we make our way to the front door, I can see inside from the large open windows. It looks quaint but

sophisticated at the same time. I gather it's Italian from
how it is decorated inside with the red pepper and cheese
shakers that are placed at each table.

Inside, Matthew lets the hostess know he has a reservation for two.

He made a reservation for us.

The thought alone sends familiar chills sliding down my
arms. The hostess leads us to a small table in the back, just
a two-seater. It's pressed in the corner with a dimly lit light
on the wall next to it.

"Here you are," she says. "Your server will be right with
you," she adds with a pleasant look.

We sit across from each other and pick up the menus.

"I hope you like Italian," he says.

"I *am* Italian," I say, peaking over my menu with an open
smile. "I can't wait to try this place."

Realistically, few things in life make me happy. Staying
busy, sushi, sex, and *Italian food*. Throw in my favorite
person, Lauren, and your girl is *thrilled*. So I'm truly happy to be here. The only looming thought in my mind right
now is how the man of my dreams in front of me is going
to *eat*.

I peek at him over my menu to stare at him, praying to
whatever god that will listen that he doesn't chew with his
mouth open. He's perfect in every way. His tousled hair,

the 'almost not noticeable today' stubble covering the lower part of his face. The way his lips remain full even when closed together. His cupids bow looks to have a really thin scar on one side. His blazing brown eyes. Maybe I could look past him chewing with his mouth open, I just...won't ever eat with him for the rest of our lives, and we can remain in perfect bliss together. I'm trying to convince myself, but I'm not sure it's working.

"I think I'm going to get the Chicken Parmesan," he says as he closes his menu.

"Do you like bruschetta?" I close mine.

"I do," he smiles.

"Do you want to split that?"

"Sure. Is that all you're going to eat?"

"No." I smile. I forgot he doesn't know me well yet, nor does he know the fact that I can put away some food. Usually, when Lo and I find a new restaurant, we order four staple dishes off the menu and split everything. It's a way we get to try the menu quickly to decide our favorites. "I was going to get the Chicken Piccata too." I place my menu on top of his.

"Can I have a Pinot Noir, please," I say, tilting my chin up to the waiter who just arrived.

"Water is fine for me," Matthew says.

"You're eating Italian food with *no wine*?" I ask him jokingly.

He laughs slightly and says, "I don't really like to drink. I did enough of it when I was younger. It got me into a lot of trouble, so if I do now, it's a *very rare* occasion."

I sit in awe and ask him about his life growing up in Boston.

"My brother and I, like I told you, grew up in foster care. I only remember bits and pieces about my mom, but it was enough to know she loved drugs more than her kids."

"I'm sorry," I say as I drop my eyes to the table.

I didn't mean to interject, but the thought of his words stabs my heart. How could a mother or a father completely neglect their child? A human *they* created. It's hard for me to wrap my mind around because the love my parents showed me was constant. I couldn't imagine it being the total opposite for someone so young.

"It is what it is," he says, looking almost sympathetic for *me*. Like he's sorry I have to hear about his drug-addicted mother.

"Well," he continues. "Having to go from home to home really affected my brother and me, I think. We would ditch school all the time, stay out late, and party with the older kids. We were only about thirteen and fourteen when we started drinking." He looks disappointed in himself.

"Anyways, like I said — I did a lot of bad shit, but the day I met the Birch's is really when I think my life turned around. They pushed me to do better in school. They told me I could be anything I wanted to be when I got older. I remember begging and pleading to them to let me stay at their house, but unfortunately, they couldn't get licensed for foster care quickly enough. By that time, I was already eighteen. I told them I wanted to become a doctor and help people, especially trauma patients. They helped put me through med school, and that's about it," he says, fully grinning from ear to ear.

I was worried that talking about it would make him sad because of how dark his past seemed. I almost stopped him because I didn't want him to be upset the rest of the evening. I'm sure it's hard to talk about. He dealt with a lot of heavy things at such a young age. No child should be put in that type of situation.

Hearing the way he speaks about Bill and Caroline warms my heart. I can feel my eyes start to become glossy but I inhale through my nose to relax.

Our waiter brings our drinks out and takes our food order as we continue divulging into our jobs, and I learn that he only has a few more months of his residency before he becomes an attending. I watch, fascinated with him. The way his Adam's apple moves when he speaks makes me wonder if that's what causes his voice to sound low and gruff.

"So, you're not married and *far* from it?" I ask, repeating what he told me in the bookstore today.

"Yes." He laughs. "I haven't really dated anyone for a couple of years," he tells me. "*You're* not married, are you?" he asks now in a full grin.

"I'm also *far* from it." I laugh while placing my napkin on my lap.

"I find that hard to believe," he says. Bringing his mouth from an open smile to a closed one.

"Why's that?"

"Well, for one, you're stunning. When I asked you out, I thought you would say no because you were already taken."

"Are you happy I'm not?"

"Very." He brings the ends of his lips in a curl even higher.

"You're not too bad looking yourself, Matthew," I say, returning the compliment. Playing his words in my head over and over.

you're stunning
you're stunning
you're stunning

Our appetizer arrives as we continue the conversation. Now, it's the moment of truth. I keep telling myself it's fine if he chews loudly. That's fine. I'll just — get earplugs out at dinner time. Or I'll undergo hypnotherapy and get over this small case of misophonia if that's what I even have.

He looks excited to try it.

Shit, maybe I should just excuse myself to the bathroom while he eats. Dammit, that would be noticeable, and what if I come back too early and I see him at the table chomping so wide the food falls out of his mouth. *Ugh*. What is wrong with me? He's raising the piece of bread to his mouth as I look at him. I try to look at the plate of food in front of me, but it's like my eyes have to see what's going to happen even though my heart doesn't want to. And here he goes. Food in his mouth and....

Nothing.

Closed mouth.

No loud sounds.

Oh my god.

Fucking jackpot.

I smile as I grab a piece of the toasted bread for myself.

We enjoy the rest of our dinner, I try to let him know we can split the tab, but he thoroughly insists on paying. I don't argue long. It's nice to have been on an actual date that I enjoyed with the only man I would really want to be on one with anyways.

As we make our way back to the car, I find it a little difficult to walk in my heels. I did have three glasses of wine, but that was because of *first date nerves*, *how's he going to chew nerves*, and *just being in front of him nerves*.

During the drive, he talks to me, keeping me occupied while occasionally squeezing my hand if he gets a glimpse of my eyes closed.

We round the corner, and I can tell we're coming up to my house.

"Where should I park?" Matthew asks as I slowly open my eyes.

"Just up there is fine," I state, noticing there isn't any close parking by my door.

I know he is going to offer to walk me to my door, but I can't risk it — I need to say goodbye right now. If we have any chance at all, I need to take things slow with him.

"I had a really great time tonight," I say to him as I shift my body to face his, leaning towards the center console.

"So did I. Let me walk you to your door."

I knew it.

"Matt." I sigh, leaning just a bit further into him. "I don't mean to be too forward. But I don't think we should have sex until we've had at least five dates."

It sounded better in my head because the way it came out of my mouth felt odd, and I can tell by the way he's looking at me, he's thoroughly confused. He's smiling, though... I mean awkwardly, like the embarrassed smile I gave him at the bookstore.

"Five dates?" he asks, still with a questionable look but a *very* attractive grin

"Five dates," I state with an assured nod, more confident in my decision.

"Okay." He smirks as he leans even closer to me, minimizing the space between us. If I were to stretch my neck out just a little further, our lips would be touching right now.

He places his hand on the side of my face, threading his fingers into my hair, and asks, "What about kissing?" He brushes his thumb over my bottom lip.

"You can kiss my cheek." I smile softly, almost whispering into his mouth.

"Five dates, no kissing on the lips. I think I can do that," he says back to me in the same soft tone I did. I can feel the heat from his breath on me, and it's taking everything I have not to reach out and plant my mouth on his.

"Thank you," I say as I lean slightly past his mouth and gently kiss his cheek. I can feel the stubble beneath my lips, making me crave him even more.

"Wait right here," he says as he slowly backs away, releasing his hand from my face while keeping my gaze. He gets out of the car and rounds the front to open my door, extending his hand toward me.

"Can I walk you to the door?"

I take his hand and step out.

"If you get anywhere near my door, I'm afraid I'll be forced to grab you by the shirt and pull you in." I laugh.

"Then I better wait here," he says as he kisses the top of my hand and leans his back on his car to watch me walk away.

I release my hand from his and take a couple of steps backward, only to keep our gaze intact. The way he's leaning on his car with his arms crossed, eyeing me up and down. This is one of those moments where I'd be taking a thousand photos if I had a camera in my head.

CHAPTER ELEVEN

L auren's favorite color is yellow, which I guess is why Carter made an archway full of lemon leaves and real lemons as the staple of their proposal. It looked better on FaceTime than it did in my head when he explained the idea months ago. It was beautiful, and of course, Lauren cried. She was excited to show me her ring even though I helped pick it out. She was proud I could keep a secret that long, which made us both giggle.

That was the most exciting thing to happen at work today. Other than me reorganizing Bill's desk that I just finished. I don't think it's ever been cleaned before, and he was so happy the entire time I did it. His face lit up, almost like the Santa Clause you see in the movies with rosy cheeks.

"Vivy helped me clean my desk." I hear Bill say to Caroline from the back. I love that they both call me that. My mom used to call me Vivy when I was little. I hadn't heard it in so long that I forgot about it until the first day it came out of Caroline's mouth. Floods of memories came swarming to me, and I had to step out and wipe the tear that was falling onto my cheek.

"Oh, how sweet of you." Caroline emerges from the back, swinging the curtain open.

"It's my pleasure, honestly. It'll be much easier for you both to find everything you're looking for. And I've already finished stock and ordering today," I say with a smile.

"Listen, Vivy. We're having our Grandson over for dinner this evening. Would you like to join us?" she asks with vibrant eyes and a sinister grin like she's up to something. "I'm making lasagna!"

"I would love to, Caroline," I say with a chuckle.

I didn't know they had any grandchildren. I really didn't even know they had *children*. I would assume it would have come up in the many talks Bill and I had. "What time should I be over?"

"Dinner will be done at six o'clock, dear. I'll write down our address for you. Bill will be so happy. It was his idea," she says with that same grin.

I finish my shift after only another hour, which gives me plenty of time to get home and freshen up before going to their house.

My feelings of nervousness take over on my walk home. I already don't like meeting new people, especially if I'm sober, and figuring out how old Bill and Caroline are, their grandson may be around the same age as me. I don't want to miss out on meeting more of their family, but I hope they are not trying to set me up. I'm not sure how I can politely tell them I'm already interested in someone and I have to wait for at least four more dates to decide if I'm totally compatible with.

Let's be real. You could have the man of your dreams right in front of you, but if he screws you like some fucked up jackhammer, those feelings can fade. *And fast*.

Thinking of Matt, I realize I haven't heard from him since our last date. He did say he was working today, but maybe me being to presumptuous scared him away. I should have just shut my mouth and let whatever happen, happen. I just wanted to get to know him better before diving that deep. Thinking, if he thought I was too easy, maybe that would deter him. Or the same thought, if he's horrible in bed, then whatever we have now will be gone. I just want to keep it intact for as long as possible.

Once I get home, I run upstairs to my bedroom to look for something to wear. After about an hour and a half of going through my closet, I end up sitting on the floor, defeated. On the ground of my bedroom— shirts, dresses, pants, and shoes are sprawled out *everywhere*. I must have tried on over fifteen different outfits, mix and matching, trying to find the perfect combination. Nothing. And I mean *nothing,* is fitting right, or so it seems. I don't know why I'm so worked up anyway. It's just dinner. A casual dinner. I'm too wound up to even focus, so I run downstairs and pour a glass of wine to sip on to try to calm some nerves.

The sip of wine I was supposed to have accidentally turned into me chugging it, which is fine, considering I have only thirty minutes to get dressed and fix my hair before I have to leave. As I run upstairs, I hear my phone ping from my bedroom. My lock screen says —

Matthew: What are you doing later? I'd like to see you.

I'm thankful I haven't scared him off yet, but I'm running out of time, so I toss my phone back on the bed and throw on a soft green dress that compliments my olive skin. It has a sweetheart neckline, ideally not the first choice because of my cleavage showing, but it's too late now, and with only minutes to spare, I quickly run a brush through my hair before I dart out of the door.

Bill and Caroline's house is an extra ten minutes from the bookstore, but thankfully, it isn't fall yet, so the evening weather is still nice enough for such a long stroll.

As I come up to Caroline's address, I see a cozy white cottage with dark green shutters. It's lined with perfectly trimmed bushes out front. I walk up to the door and knock. Bill is the one to answer, and his eyes widen with joy as he sees me.

"Caroline!" He shouts to her as I walk in, "Vivy's here!"

I hear Caroline cheer from the kitchen and take my shoes off at the front door before Bill walks me to the dining room.

"Sit, Sit!" Caroline exclaims as she emerges from the kitchen, holding a large pan with her oven mitts.

I've seen them in work mode at the store plenty of times. It's nice to see them at home, in their natural habitat. Caroline is wearing an apron over her blue knit sweater with a smile bigger than I've ever seen plastered on her face.

Their dining table is a beautiful oak with a white lace tablecloth resting on top. Dishes are placed at four of the six seats, and for a second, I completely forgot about the extra company joining us tonight. I was in my thoughts as

I came to the house, taking in their home's different sights and smells. Whoever is the Birch's grandson is one lucky bastard. I would have killed for this growing up.

"Vivian, would you like something to drink?" Bill asks as he sits at the head of the table.

"I've got wine!" Caroline shouts from the kitchen

"She's been drinking since we locked up the store." He laughs.

"Wine would be great!" I tell Caroline.

As she brings me a full stemmed glass, she sits next to Bill. "Our grandson should be here any minute. He was just getting off work when I spoke to him," she says.

"I didn't know you two had kids," I say while taking a sip of my wine.

Pinot Noir, great taste Caroline, great taste.

"We don't," Bill says as he looks at Caroline seated next to him. "Matthew isn't technically our grandson, but we would love him just as much if he was."

Matthew.

"You've met him, I think, haven't you, Vivy? In the store. Well, that was, gee, how long ago was that, Bill?" Caroline asks, passing glances between both Bill and me.

"How long ago since what?" he snaps jokingly.

The way Bill and Caroline talk to each other is somewhat comical. Bill is always a smart ass to her, not in a mean way; it's hilarious. He is always giving her shit. Whether it's her age, her memory, you name it, he'll tease her for it. It's all in good fun, though, and she always zings him right back. I love to see it play out. It makes me hope if I ever have a husband one day, that we can still banter well into our eighties.

"Since Vivian's first week with us. Don't get me started, Bill. I'll put you in a home next year," she teases.

I laugh with them, but it's sinking in that *Matt* will be here. Were they trying to set me up with him all along? Is this even a setup? I don't know, and frankly don't have time to care before the doorbell rings.

"Come in!" Bill shouts in his shaky voice.

In walks Matt with a gray sweatshirt on and familiar jeans.

"Vivian. What are you doing here?" he asks with that fantastic smile of his.

"You two *do* know each other," Bill says, raising his eyebrows up and down at Caroline as she slaps his shoulder teasingly.

Matt takes a seat right next to me. He sits taller than I do, so I know for a fact every time he looks at me, he can see the tops of my breasts peeking out from my dress. I don't mind, though, *at all*.

"Sorry, I'm late. I was supposed to be off work an hour ago. It's been a hectic day," he states apologetically to all of us. "I didn't know you were going to be here, Viv," he says while tapping me with his elbow.

"Bill thought it would be nice to bring you two together," Caroline says, holding her wine glass with two hands by her chin, her grin beaming from behind it.

"Damnit, Caroline, it was supposed to be our secret!" Bill teases.

We dive into Caroline's *delicious* lasagna and pass the warm rolls around. Bill and Caroline tell us stories from when they were together in their twenties, and I relish in the dinner, it's been so long since I've had a good home-cooked meal. My dad knew how to cook some things, but my mom was a *fantastic* cook. Unfortunately, she didn't get to teach *me* how to cook before she passed, so I'm stuck in my adult life ordering takeout most of the time.

"So Vivy, what do you want to do with your life? Surely you don't want to work for us forever." Caroline giggles.

"Well, I would love to own a bookstore one day like you guys," I say, smiling as I take another sip of my pinot. "I've been trying to save for years, but it seems like no matter what, I'll just never be ready."

"Why not?" Bill asks.

"It's expensive. And it's just a dream. Besides, it would be a little frightening running my own business," I say, shrugging my shoulders and letting out a nervous laugh.

"Be afraid, Viv, then do it anyway," Bill says with a soft grin. This must be another *Bill Birch Life Quote* but I kind of like it.

"Matthew, how's work going?" Caroline asks.

"Work is — busy." Matt sighs. "But it's rewarding." When he talks about his job, his face changes. It moves from this kind of tense gratitude. Like, despite the stress of it, he'd never give it up. The longer I consider it, the more my own doubt creeps in.

What do I have to offer him, really? In terms of career, he's miles ahead of me, and I don't know if I can ever just forget that.

As if he can read my mind, he places his hand on my knee underneath the table.

I must have gasped at the sensation of his touch because the Birch's directions are fixated on me now.

"Did you know I actually met Matthew at his work?" I say nervously, trying to cover up the incident. Quickly bringing the wine to my lips and taking a gulp.

"Well, not at work," I continue nervously as I release the glass from my lips.

"Viv's car was the one that hit mine in the accident I had a couple of months ago," Matt interjects after realizing I'm fumbling over my words.

"What a small world," Caroline says.

"A small world indeed," Bill replies.

Matt glides his hand further up my thigh under the table.

Jesus, What is he trying to do right now? He must not know that his little touch sends signals throughout my body, all pointing to my *V.*

My poor vagina.

Hasn't seen the touch of a man in at least two months. Completely to long for my patterns of behavior. Maybe that's why she's crying out at every minuscule feeling of his skin on mine.

I glance at him as he traces his thumb on my thigh. He's going to have to stop eventually because having wet panties at the Birch's is not what I had planned on the agenda for this evening.

As we finish up, Caroline clears the table for a card game. I offered to help, but she insisted I stay put.

"Does this count as a second date?" Matthew whispers in my ear as he gives my thigh a tight squeeze.

I give him a slight smile before Caroline comes back with a deck of cards, a paper plate, and dollar bills.

What the fuck do we need a paper plate for?

"It's called Thirty-One!" Bill shouts as he passes out the cards. Apparently, in this game — the goal is to get your cards totaling as close to thirty-one as you can, all in the same suit, of course. It takes me only a couple of rounds to catch on, but thankfully for this game, you need *two* hands. At least my underwear can get dry before I stand up.

We spend an hour and a half playing before we call it a night. After thanking Caroline and Bill for having me over and saying goodbye with hugs to both, Matt and I exit the door simultaneously.

"Let me take you home," he says as we stand outside on the Birch's porch. "It's dark. I don't want you walking alone."

I take an audible breath and reluctantly agree, closing my eyes most of the time he drives.

"Can I walk you to your door tonight?" Matt says as we park near my house.

I nod yes, even though I know what trouble this will bring me. But the way Caroline's heavy-handed pours are getting to me, my body is screaming for him. I've just to take it slow, that's all.

Take it slow, Vivian.

"Can you help me inside?" I say with innocent eyes as we stand in front of my door.

"Is it going to break your five-date rule?" he asks curiously with a grin.

"Nope," I giddily reply.

I open my front door, throw my keys down, and turn around to face him in my living room.

"Can you help me unzip this dress? It was hard to get on myself," I say, looking up at him, our bodies close to each other.

"Turn around," he says with an upward nod.

"Upstairs." I point. "In my bedroom."

"Lead the way." He gives me a sly smile.

I know what I'm doing, I think. This doesn't break my rule. Right? It'll be a testament to me, too, knowing I can control myself. Knowing I can stop myself and stick to my word.

We get up to my bedroom, and I grab a T-shirt and a pair of shorts from my closet, dropping them on the bed and standing directly in front of Matt with my back to him. I slowly toss my hair over my shoulder, giving him an unobstructed view of my lengthy zipper and exposing my neck to him.

He reaches his hands up and slowly grabs it. As the zipper moves down, my dress shows more and more of my back for him. His fingertips graze against my skin, causing icy chills to form at the tops of my shoulders, running down to my hands. I can feel his hot breath on my neck, standing so close to me. I feel the tug of the zipper stop even though I wish this could go on for hours. I know how low the zipper goes, and he brought it down to the end. It's exposing the top of my black lacy thong.

He pauses, with his hand still on my zipper. I can feel him lean closer into me, causing me to tilt my head, exposing *even more* for him. I feel his mouth kiss the base of my neck, forcing me to roll my eyes in pleasure and throw my head back unwillingly.

"It's not your lips," he whispers in my ear.

I can't argue with that logic.

He places another kiss on my neck, lower than the first, as he brings both hands up to meet the sleeves of my dress. Pushing them down slightly to expose more skin. He places his mouth on me again, even lower, working his way to my shoulder.

He moves his hand up to sweep my hair away from the back of my neck, placing his mouth on me once more. This time, I can feel his hot tongue graze my skin, which sends an involuntary moan to escape from my mouth.

He can tell how my body is reacting to his touch, and he takes one step closer, pushing his body flush against mine. I can feel him growing underneath his jeans as he presses into me further.

He dives in for another kiss on my neck, just below my ear, laying his tongue flat against me as he puckers his lips around it. I moan again, bringing my right arm up to grab the back of his neck, pushing him to kiss me again. He does so, and I shove my ass back onto him, forcing us to be even closer, if that's possible. I can feel his cock, rock solid against me.

"I want to taste you, Vivian," he groans softly against my neck.

"Five dates," I whimper as I throw my head back, rolling my hips into him again to make him continue.

He grabs my right hand and guides it to my thigh, kissing me once more on my neck as he moves my hand under my dress.

"Play with yourself," he whispers in his gruff voice, still resting his hand on top of mine as he guides my fingers to push my panties to the side.

I do as I'm told, dipping my fingers to my entrance and spreading my wetness over my clit before I circle it lightly. Groaning against him as he presses his rigid tongue on my earlobe, biting at it softly. He pulls my hand away, bringing it up to meet his mouth. Only taking a moment before his lips wrap around my fingers, and he drags his tongue against them. Moaning softly as he tastes.

"Jesus, Vivian." He sighs into my ear.

Hearing his words sends my body shock waves, and in an instant, I reach my arm behind me to grab onto his jeans, running my hand along the length of his cock. He pushes into me as if for me to keep going.

I need to stop, if I don't stop now, I'll regret not giving...whatever this is between us a real chance, and I don't want to break the promise to myself either.

I turn around to face him, my cheeks flushed and my body hot. I look up at him and hesitate before I say, "We have to stop."

"I know," he groans.

"I don't want to," I plea.

He leans into me, pressing his forehead against mine. "We have to. Three more dates." *his heavy breath, hot on my lips.* "What are you doing for breakfast, lunch, and dinner tomorrow?"

CHAPTER TWELVE

*O**h, Matt.* Keep going. Please keep going. Oh, you're gonna make me come.

He leans in and moans, "Your alarm is going off."

My eyes peel open as the light pours into my room from the sunrise.

SHIT.

I was dreaming. Why couldn't I finish that dream? That *fucking* alarm.

Today's my day off, so before Matt reluctantly left my house last night, he told me he wanted to cook me breakfast. He took my phone and said he was setting an alarm, and when I wake up, I need to get dressed and head over. He also said he was going to write his address somewhere downstairs, but I haven't bothered to look yet because that *fucking* alarm is still going off.

I need coffee, STAT.

I head downstairs and grab two Tylenol while starting a pot. Caroline must have had expensive wine last night because that seems to be when I get the worst hangovers. My body's used to cheap alcohol.

I see that Matt did leave his address, too, right on my grocery list. I type it into my phone to see how far away it is before I grab a cup of coffee and head upstairs to change.

I pull out a navy sweatshirt and white cotton shorts from my closet before brushing my teeth and grabbing my white baseball cap.

He lives twenty-two minutes away on foot which is great for me to get some exercise in. I keep my phone in my hand as a text rings through.

Matthew: Pancakes or waffles?
Me: You choose
Matthew: I'll make both.

I don't even know what emotions are flowing through my body right now while walking to his house. Replaying last night, I don't see how, in any way, shape, or form, this man is bad in bed. My body is still chilled from his touch.

I walk through the Market District to get to his building. From the sidewalk looking up, it's hard to tell how tall it is. It seems to go on forever. Gray, lined with nothing but windows.

The lobby is massive, with dark wood floors and tall hanging chandeliers. Glass artworks line the walls where the windows are not, and chestnut leather chairs are placed throughout by glass tables.

This place is *chic*. I snap a couple of pictures and send them to Lauren. She loves shit like this. Classy and elegant architecture. I would be happy in a motel, but I guess that's why our friendship works.

Opposites attract, right?

The concierge points me in the direction of the elevators, and I get in, pressing the button to the fourteenth floor. I step off and follow the signs to **1415**. Knocking on the door as I arrive. The butterflies in my stomach are circling around as I wait for him to open up.

"Good morning," Matthew says as he swings the door open while mixing a large bowl of batter with a wooden spoon. There is flour dusted on the right side of his chin as he grins at me. "Come in. It's not done yet."

I walk closely behind him, moving through the short hallway. It opens up to his living room and kitchen, which is lined with floor-to-ceiling windows in the corner. His kitchen is sleek, with gray slate cabinets and white marble countertops that are hard to see because of the mess. Flour and cracked eggs coat the bowls and utensils sprawled out on the center island.

"Need some help?" I laugh as he makes his way to the stove.

"I should warn you; I'm not the *best* cook," he says while pouring the batter from his bowl onto a hot pan.

"Neither am I." *I laugh.* "We'll be screwed if we ever get married."

I giggle nervously, embarrassed that those words just came out of my mouth. My embarrassment quickly fades as he chuckles back.

I take a seat on the barstool, watching him flip what looks to be an odd-shaped pancake.

"Do you want chocolate chips in your pancakes?" he asks with his back facing me.

"Sure!" I say excitedly.

"Orange juice or water?" he asks, still flipping pancakes. "That's all I have right now."

"Orange juice is good. I can get it. Where are your cups?"

He points to the cabinet closest to the refrigerator.

"What do you want to drink?" I ask.

"Orange juice is good for me too." He glances over with a smile.

I fill both cups halfway with juice and place them on the small circle dining table in the corner of the room. It has one chair on each side with a grey wooden bowl filled with bright green apples in the center.

"Pancakes are done," he announces as I walk towards the kitchen area, grabbing the plate of stacked pancakes from him and bringing them back to the table. Only a few look a bit burnt. "There's a fruit bowl in the fridge if you want to grab that." He points.

I grab the large bowl and shut the refrigerator door with my foot. At the same time, Matthew takes a plate of waffles over to the table.

"If it's terrible, we can order delivery." He scoots out my chair. I sit and laugh at his comment.

"You didn't have to do this for me," I say with a sly smile as I grab a pancake from the top of the stack.

"I wanted to."

His cooking isn't terrible, it's actually pretty decent, but it is hard to mess up a pancake. As we sit and enjoy each other's company, I can hear my phone buzzing from my pocket.

Lauren: Our family is going to come Saturday for an engagement dinner. Carter and I already booked the house next door for you. You're coming too. You

can check in at noon. I'll email you the deets. Love you.

Shit Lauren. That's a four-hour car ride. How in the hell am I going to do that?

"Everything okay?" Matt says, noticing the anxiety washing over my face.

I take a deep sigh. "I have to go to The Hamptons this weekend."

"You're upset because...you have to go to The Hamptons?"

"Lauren and Carter rented a house for me on the beach this weekend for their engagement dinner," I continue, setting my phone down on the table.

"You're upset because...you get to stay in a beach house...for free...in The Hamptons?" He shakes his head, still not understanding where the disappointment in my voice is coming from.

"I have to drive." I sigh, dropping my head into my hands, and burying my face in them.

"Do you want me to drive you?" he asks after a couple of moments of silence.

I peek my eyes through my fingers as I hear his words.

"Can you?" I ask with a soft voice

"I don't have to work this weekend. I don't mind taking you."

I sigh, releasing some of my tension. "Would you like to go to The Hamptons this weekend for my friend's engagement dinner?" I officially ask in a sweet tone.

"I'd love to," he says, bringing his glass of orange juice to his lips.

After breakfast, I help him clean up the mess in the kitchen, getting to work with a paper towel and disinfecting spray in my hands. I watch him stand over the sink, washing each dish by hand. When he picks up a plate, the muscles in his arms contract. Picking up the smaller plates, I can see how big his hands actually are. It sinks in that he and I will be alone, *really alone*, overnight in a beach house. Those butterflies in the pit of my belly swirl again, and for once since the accident, I think I can stomach the drive.

Matthew's phone rings from the corner bedroom. He quickly finds a towel to dry his hands and darts off. I can hear him mumbling but can't make out any words.

"Vivian!" he calls.

I follow his voice around the corner to see him standing next to his bed, lifting his shirt over his head.

Oh my god, his body.

"I got called into work," he groans. "I've got to take a quick shower, but I might be there all night," he says while rummaging through his closet. "You're more than welcome to stay, but I don't want to force you."

"Oh," I say quietly, "That's okay!" I exclaim. "I should try to find some sort of gift to bring this weekend anyways."

"Sit." He points to his bed in front of me. "I'll walk you out."

He moves past me and into his bathroom, swinging the door shut, but it doesn't close all of the way. I sit on the edge of his bed and fold my hands in my lap. I can see him somewhat behind the door through the tiny bit of space he left open. He starts the shower, and I can hear the water run. I see what looks to be him pulling down his pants and boxers at the same time, his tanned skin peeking through the crack. Jesus, why can't the door be open a little more?

I remain seated for only a couple of minutes, trying to get any little peak I can of him standing behind the glass before I hear the water shut off. I can slightly see him get out of the shower, but the view is quickly obstructed by a white towel.

The door thrusts open as he stands in the door frame. The water droplets drip from his body still. His wet hair looks pitch black, and the strands of his tresses reach past his eyebrows. He walks towards me, holding the towel around his waist, and securing it with his hand. As he stands directly in front of me, I tilt my chin up to look at his face. He cradles my cheek softly with his free hand and kisses my forehead in the center. "I'm glad we got to eat breakfast together," he whispers to me as his face is still close to mine.

"Me too," I whisper back, watching him pull his head back to meet my eyes with his hand still on my face.

"Mind if I get changed?" he says while releasing his hand from me, and taking a couple of steps backward.

"Not at all," I reply.

He keeps my gaze locked in, bringing the towel around his waist up to his hair, vigorously rubbing it back and forth, then moving the towel to dry his chest and arms. He drops the towel on his floor, and there he is. Standing stark naked in front of me. The way his muscles run down, forming a V shape from his hips looks like it was carved by the gods. I can feel my jaw clench as he keeps his stare. My insides warming as I look at him. I swallow hard as my heart starts to race. He walks forward, leaning to the side of me to grab the clothes he had picked out.

"Did this count as a date?" I ask as he slowly dresses.

He smirks. "I'd like to think so."

I let him finish changing — gathering everything he needs for work before he walks me down to the lobby. Replaying what his naked body looked like over and over inside my head.

"I'll get ahold of you when I get off," he says as he kisses my cheek. I nod, and we exit the building together.

"Goodbye, Vivian," he says, holding his eyes with mine as he walks back towards the parking garage.

"Thanks for breakfast," I reply while doing the same in the opposite direction towards my house.

He finally rounds the corner to where I can't see him, and I spin around to walk forward, releasing my pent-up nerves with a sigh.

Why does he have to be so *damn* gorgeous? And why in the hell did I have to make up some stupid silly rule about not having sex with the gorgeous man until five fucking dates.

I'm an idiot, *that's why*.

Lauren will just get a kick at this; I know it. I can't wait to tell her when she's home, but this is *her* week, so I'll let her relish in it until she's back to reality.

I get home and set down the brown bags of fresh produce I grabbed along the way. I hadn't grocery shopped in a while, so it was probably best I did that on my one free day this week. On the way home, I also grabbed Lauren and Carter's engagement gift from a local store. I had a hard time choosing, so I just decided on a bottle of Chardonnay with a minimalist label that reads *Wedding Planning Wine* paired with two wine glasses, engraved with Mr. & Mrs. I also purchased a large wooden box with golden crinkle confetti to house them in. My phone dings from my purse as I'm putting my groceries away.

Lauren: I can't wait to see you!! You will love it here, the beach is so beautiful.

Me: I can't wait! Can I bring Matt?

Lauren: Absolutely!

Me: Good cause I already invited him.

Lauren: I'm so glad the house next door is one bedroom.

Oh. God.

It's fine. I can sleep in the same bed without touching him. It'll be *just* fine. It's not like I've dreamed about having dirty hot sex with him since the day I met him.

Jesus, Viv, get a grip. It's cool. We're cool. Everything's *chill*.

CHAPTER THIRTEEN

B ill isn't feeling well, so he stayed home from work
today. It's quiet without him. Too quiet. I didn't
realize how much I would miss his banter with Caroline
or him calling me into his office to help with his computer.
The last time he called me in there, he didn't know how to
exit out of a tab, I told him to press the 'red x' in the top
left — he thought I was a genius. It made me giggle, but
silly things like that make him very easily missed.

I've got two days to get my shit together before taking a
road trip with Matt. I looked at the house Lauren set up.
It's stunning, of course. The perfect place for romantic,
steamy sex.

None of which I'll be having.

I've already organized all the new titles we got today
and made some marketing flyers for Birch Books. *Alana*

Debose, an up-and-coming author, will do a book signing here next month, which will be *great* for business.

Since I've finished all my duties today, I ask Caroline if she is okay with me leaving early and bringing Bill some soup from his favorite cafe next door. She happily agrees, and out the door I go.

"Potato bacon to go," I tell the cashier at Wiskers Cafe. This *joint,* as Bill likes to call it, was originally owned by his best friend, Robert. He said they both bought the commercial spaces right next to each other on a whim. Robert passed away, and his children run the business now, but Bill swears it's still the exact same recipe from fifty years ago. I haven't tried it yet, but today seems like the day to change that. "Make it two, please!"

Caroline had already called Bill to let him know I was coming and to leave the door unlocked, so when I walked up the stairs to his porch, I knocked once, then let myself in.

"Vivy," Bill says as he slowly lifts out of his recliner.

"Sit, Bill! I brought you some soup," I grin while holding up the large paper bag.

"Oh!" he says with an open smile, throwing his hands on his cheeks.

"Where are your bowls?" I ask as I place the bag on the coffee table. Bill tells me where I can find them, and after looking in the wrong place five times, I finally get them. I grab two bowls and two spoons and make my way back to the living room. I pour our soups and grab two tv trays, setting one in front of Bill, and another in front of the recliner next to him, so I can sit near him.

Family Feud is on, and you would think Bill had never seen the show before the way he is laughing. We start shouting our answers at the TV screen, cheering when our answer shows on the board. On commercial breaks, he tells me more about his life, where he grew up, and what his parents did for work, and I divulge the same. He lets me know he and Caroline have always wanted children, but no matter how many times they tried, it wasn't in the cards for them. He asks if I want children of my own, which I tell him I do...and plenty of them. He lets me know that he hopes to be around when the time comes so he can meet them. After we finish eating, I bring our dishes to the kitchen and wash them by hand, putting the bowls and utensils back in the same spot. It's almost four o'clock, and I should head back to help Caroline close the store.

"I would hug you, but I don't want to get your cooties," I joke with Bill as he laughs.

"Vivy, you really made my day," he says back with an endearing smile.

I motion an air hug to him from the front door and make my way back to the store to close up with Caroline so she can get home early tonight to be with Bill.

After work on my walk home, I think about how different my life was a couple of months ago. Who knows where I would have been if I didn't get into a car accident? The next day, I would have gone out and applied for jobs...Birch Books wasn't hiring until four weeks after. I wouldn't have met Bill and Caroline, and I certainly wouldn't have met *Matthew*.

I get home and run upstairs to change into my pajamas, rifling through my drawers, trying to find anything at this point. I forgot to do laundry, per usual, so my black slip dress is what will have to do. It's comfortable in how the silk touches my skin but not how the lacy demi cups barely cover my nipples.

I go into my bathroom and throw my hair up with a claw clip before I scoot into my pink fuzzy slippers and head back downstairs to order delivery while I pop open a bottle of wine.

On my second glass, I realize I completely forgot to order Uber Eats. Searching through the app, I decide that a small Margherita pizza is calling my name.

I place the order and turn on some music before walking to the mirror hanging by my stairs. I can see my cheeks are flushed from the wine, like a natural rouge. I run my hand over my cheeks to feel their warmth while dragging my fingers down to trace the left side of my jawline. My fingers feel soft against my skin, so I drag them further down, gently tracing my collarbone while taking another sip of wine from the glass in my right hand. I lightly touch the lace pattern right above my nipple, then bring my fingers down to the large slit on my left leg. I stand there, drawing my fingers slowly and softly along the split hem when suddenly, my doorbell rings. Assuming it's the pizza I just ordered — the instructions I left in the notes clearly state *leave by door*. There's no need for me to get it now. I stay standing in place, looking at myself in the mirror, when my doorbell rings again.

What in the *hell* dude?

I move my wine glass to my left hand and swing open the door. Completely forgetting I'm essentially undressed for the delivery driver, I gasp when I find Matthew standing in front of me with dark blue scrubs on.

He grins. *That fucking grin*. With his perfect pearl-white teeth showing.

The music is playing rather loudly, and neither Matt nor I are saying any words. He just grins, and I just *gawk*. My jaw dropped wide.

"Are you having a party?" He laughs.

"I was until you showed up," I tease.

"I had a little break. I wanted to see you." He takes a step closer to me. I look up at him and smile with my lips pressed together.

"You look flushed." He grins while hooking my chin with his index finger and gliding his thumb over the bottom of my cheek.

"It's the wine," I say softly.

"And *this*..." he says as he moves his hand gently to my shoulder, running his finger down the strap of my slip. "I want you to wear it this weekend."

I swallow the lump in my throat as I take in his touch. He leans into me as he whispers, "Get back to touching yourself in the mirror, but make sure you're thinking about me this time."

A chill runs between my legs, knowing I'm getting wetter by the second. My heart is pounding in my chest, and just as soon as he arrived here, he leaves.

What. The. Hell.

What in the name of all things holy just happened? I shut my door hastily and press my back against it. The quick motion spilled some wine on my floor, but I'm too flustered to give a damn. I stay leaning on my door for a minute until my doorbell rings again. What does he want now, to terrorize me some more? I swing my door open again, more sexually frustrated than I've ever been. Only to find Amal — my delivery driver taking a photo of my food, and me, on my front porch.

"Delete that," I say flatly while grabbing my pizza box and shutting the door on him.

I let out a heavy sigh and bring my food to the couch to eat while I yell at my Alexa to *shut the hell up* and stop playing music.

Friday came and went — regular duties at Birch's, and Bill's still sick, the only remotely interesting thing that happened was when Matt texted me.

Matthew: Should we just spend the night together since we have to get up early and leave tomorrow?
Me: Not a chance.

But it's Saturday now, which means Matt will be here any minute to pick me up. I grab my duffle bag and the gift before I place them by the front door. Mentally going over my checklist.

Charger. Check
Gift. Check

Underwear. Check

Slutty nightgown.......check.

My doorbell rings, and I scoop up my belongings and answer the door.

"Good morning," Matt says in a gruff voice.

"Morning." I grin.

"You got everything?"

"Yep!"

"You sure?"

"Yes, Matt."

"Black silky dress, sure?"

"I'm sure, Matt," I say, looking at him with pressed lips. He's getting a kick out of this. Pure enjoyment. He knows what he's doing. And it's not fair. Just wait until I give this fucker a taste of his own medicine.

We get in his car, and he taps in the address from my check-in instructions. Four hours and twenty minutes of drive time. Wonderful.

The home is in Montauk, I've never been, but it's Lauren and Carter's favorite spot. She face-timed me in the house they rented. The steps off the back porch lead down to the beach. If we're next door, I would imagine ours should be similar.

The home they are staying in is large enough for *both* of their families, I assume Lo decided right away I would need my own house since her brother and I briefly had a thing some years back. I haven't seen him since then, but it's a good thing she thought ahead with Matthew now as my plus one.

Along the way, I learned some things. Did you know shutting your eyes and putting your head down for an hour in a car could make you sick? Well, I didn't, but yet here we are — at ShopMart, getting me some crackers because I threw up. Could I get any sexier? He was nice about it, though. I mean, really, genuinely nice. Luckily he had an emesis bag from the hospital for some reason, so I didn't actually ruin my clothes or his car. *Thank god*. He pulled over on the highway, cars whizzing by, and held my hair...for the entire ten minutes of my hacking. Now he's inside the gas station getting me crackers and a sprite.

"I also got you ginger ale," he says while peaking his head through the driver's window that's rolled down.

"Thank you," I say with an embarrassed smile.

"Let's sit here for a bit, eat and drink everything slowly," he says while handing me the plastic bag.

"I appreciate you." I grin, and he smiles back.

"What kind of music do you like? I'll put it on while we wait."

"Anything is fine. I like everything from Post Malone to 90's country."

"George Strait?"

"Perfect." I smile while taking a sip of the Canada Dry.

We listen to a few songs before heading back on the road. Thankfully, the remaining three hours were a lot better.

When we finally pull onto Surfside Ave, it's only a short minute until we reach the house we will be staying in. Matt pulls into the drive, and from here, I can see the sand and ocean waves peaking between the houses.

I text Lauren quickly to let her know we are just pulling in. I assume the house they are staying in is to the right of us since it's quite bigger.

Our cottage is white with a wrap-around porch, looks to be two stories from the road. The white shutters and greenery lining the home pair perfectly with the large windows. I say cottage lightly. This house is bigger than the entire building I live in that houses four families.

Matt and I grab our bags from the trunk and head in. I type in the door code and open it, stepping a foot inside. The whole place is beaming with light. The entire backside has large windows overlooking the beach and ocean. The furniture is coastal but in an elegant way. The home has an open floor plan, kitchen to the left, and dining to the right. It's *spacious*, with tall ceilings and stairs off of the dining room leading up to the second floor.

"Damn," Matt says with a smile.

"Carter's an attorney," I mutter, knowing Matt is probably wondering how in the hell they could afford to rent *both* houses. This easily could go for three thousand dollars a night. My car wasn't even worth that much when I got the insurance check back.

"Let's look at the water," Matt says as he grabs my hand and quickly leads me to the large french doors that open up onto the porch. We walk towards the railing, I lean on it as he slowly wraps his arm around my waist, and we stand there. Soaking in the ocean breeze for a while.

"This is really beautiful," he says with a soft, low voice. "But not as beautiful as you." He gently kisses the side of my head.

CHAPTER FOURTEEN

"Race you up the stairs!" Matt says with a laugh.

"Matt, I'm not-" I can hardly blurt out before he starts running past me. I'm not about to let him win, so I dart after him, tugging on his shirt to slow him down. He says he won, but it was a clear tie.

We land at the top of the stairs and see another living area with a door. I walk to open it and see what's on the other side. It's an extremely large bedroom, with soft white curtains covering large doors leading out to the private porch. The linens are white with light turquoise accent pillows. Two large white button chairs sit in the corner surrounding a light wood table with hardcover books resting in the center. The natural light cases every inch of the room. The bathroom is to the right, almost as big as the bedroom itself. This is by far the nicest home I have ever stepped in. We spend a significant amount of time just searching throughout.

A little after we had arrived, Lauren called and said they had just gotten back from lunch with her family and Carter's parents. She told me to be ready and down on the beach by seven o'clock for dinner. Apparently, their favorite restaurant here agreed to cater for the evening. Carter's parents are filthy rich, so I'm sure the restaurant happily obliged at the request.

We only have about an hour until dinner now, so Matt and I have to start getting ready. I couldn't decide on what I wanted to wear tonight, so I brought two outfits.

"What about this one?" I ask Matt as I walk out of the bathroom. He's leaning on the bed, resting on his elbows, just waiting for me to come out.

"Turn around," he says while waving his finger in a circular motion. I do a slight spin, showcasing the first option. It's an olive green two-piece silk set, a small bralette for the top and a long skirt for the bottom.

"Hm...let me see it off."

I roll my eyes and smile, heading back into the bathroom to show him my second option.

"Or this?" I say as I swing the door back open, taking a couple of steps closer to him. It's a sheer black maxi dress with a cowl neck. I think it's actually a cover-up, so I paired it with back bathing suit bottoms that are slightly visible. I would add silver jewelry to this to make it fancier, but after all, we are on the beach.

"Damn," he mutters under his breath, and his eyes narrow in on all the right parts of my body.

"What? Is it bad?"

"No...not at all. I think this one is my favorite." He smiles.

Perfect, that's settled.

I start to do my makeup in the bathroom, leaving the door open so Matt can watch me from the bed. He leans on his elbow, facing me, not saying a word — only grinning from time to time.

I step out, completely finished, so Matt can change. My hair is down with the natural wave I came here with. I fixed my bangs in place to cover my scar and just added on some light makeup and mascara.

"I'll be downstairs," I yell to him while I exit the room, heading down to grab a glass of water from the kitchen.

As I fill up my glass, I hear footsteps coming down the stairs, so I stop and turn around. Matt is walking down in the khaki pants that fit him so well. His black button-down shirt isn't buttoned on the first two, showing a bit of his chest. The sunlight shining on him makes the top of his tousled hair look like a deep chestnut color. His jawline from his side profile is sharp, still visible under the stubble on his face that starts below his nose.

"You look nice," I say sweetly as he walks into the kitchen. He grabs my water glass out of my hand and takes a sip, handing it back to me with a gentle kiss on my cheek.

"Are you ready?"

"Ready as I'll ever be," I reply.

I grab Lauren and Carter's gift and head out the door, following the stone footpath to the back of the house. I can see a long table in the middle of the beach with beautiful floral centerpieces. Surrounding the table is a four-post pergola secured in the sand with lights weaving in and out of the beams and rafters. As the sky grows darker, the lights shine brighter. Lauren and her mother are standing around, who I'm assuming are Carter's parents, and it doesn't seem that Lauren's father or brother are here yet. We approach the table and say hello. Introductions are necessary since I've never met Carter's family, and no one except Lauren has met Matthew. We all take our seats as I see Lucas walk down the steps of the house onto the beach.

Lucas Atherton, also known as Lauren's brother, stands about five foot nine with short blonde hair. His jaw is tight, and he looks less childlike than he did when we had our fling. He was *good* in bed. I think that's what kept me around the longest with him because his personality was shit.

As Lucas approaches the table, he says hello to everyone and hugs Lauren. Taking a seat right next to Carter, *directly* across from me.

"Vivian," he says with a huge smile, "You look fantastic as always."

Matt clears his throat.

"This is Matt," I say, holding my hand flat, palm facing up in Matt's direction.

"Lucas," he says while reaching his hand across the table.

"Nice to meet you," Matt says flatly as he shakes his hand.

Great.

Mr. Atherton, Lauren's father, arrives, and I introduce Matt to him as well. Once everyone is seated at the table the wait staff comes around to get our drink orders.

I've never had dinner on the beach, and this is clearly an *experience.* To be waited on, in Montauk, behind our beach houses...who am I right now, Kim Kardashian?

"I'll take a vodka soda with two limes, please," I say as the waiter comes around to me.

"Water is fine for me," Matt says.

"So Vivian, what have you been up to lately? You seriously look great," Lucas says across the table as everyone engages in separate conversations.

"Just...staying busy." I ignore his compliment.

"And, Mark — was it? What do you do for a living?" Lucas asks.

"It's Matt. I work at Massachusetts General Hospital."

"He's a doctor." I grin while grabbing onto his arm.

"A doctor, huh? That's cool."

Our drinks arrive, and the first course follows. I'm not exactly sure what it is, but it's some kind of raw meat dish.

"Carpaccio," Lauren says, leaning into me, "Just try it. I promise you'll love it."

Lauren has a good sense of what I like and don't like. If she told me for a fact I would like eating Squirrel, I'd try it. I trust her judgment that much.

She was right, *it is good*.

As the night goes on, our second course comes out, then our third. By then, everyone is around three drinks in and talking over each other. Matt is laughing with Mr. Atherton, and Lauren and I are chatting about her time here. We are all in our own little worlds, enjoying the company.

"I'd like to make a toast," Mrs. Atherton says as she clinks her glass and stands, "To the future, Mr. And Mrs.

Collins, we all wish you nothing but health, happiness, and lifelong success."

We cheer and clink our glasses together, sipping our drinks before setting them back down.

Lauren is beaming, absolutely radiant. She has a long slim white dress on, it looks as shiny as silk, but the texture feels different. Her hair is in curls, halfway clipped up, and she chose her bright red lipstick tonight.

"I'm so happy for you," I squeeze her hand.

"I love you so much. Thank you for being here," she says as she leans into me to hug me from the side.

"Viv, do you remember that little restaurant we went to down by Fenway Park?" Lucas says, gazing right at me.

"Mhmm." I nod, bringing my vodka glass to my lips, not wanting to engage in this conversation *at all*.

"They took it out and put a fuckin' yoga studio there. I was hoping we would get to go back sometime soon," he says with a shit-eating grin.

Matt must want to make sure I know he's here. He traces his hand lightly from the side of my knee, following up under my dress to my thigh, keeping his hand there, resting. He must not have liked Lucas' comment.

I shiver at his touch. It's always so soft.

"It wasn't that great anyways," I say to Lucas, holding my glass in my hand and gazing at Matt with a smile.

I'm feeling buzzed, as I'm sure everyone else here is, too...besides Matt, of course. I guess I could understand his decision not to drink. He was just a child when he started, he obviously made bad decisions, so maybe he just associates alcohol with that. I hope he doesn't mind when I drink. Shit, I never even thought to ask.

The main course arrives — seared salmon with garlic and lemon sauce — or something like that, I already forgot as the waiters set the plates in front of us.

"Do you like this kind of food?" I whisper to Matt

"There's not much I won't eat," he whispers back into my ear, low and gruff-like. His sharp breath on my neck reminds me of the short night we had in my bedroom. The thought of that alone brings fire to my core. I part my legs open to cool down when Matt must take that as an invitation to go further. He moves his hand slowly to my thigh, so high that he lightly grazes his finger on the outer lining of my panties.

"Vivian," Lucas says. *Why the fuck is he still talking to me.* "Did you ever get that little tattoo lasered off like you wanted?"

He's grinning because he knows exactly what he's doing. He sees me here, with someone else, and thinks this is a perfect time to try and rekindle our three-month-long fuck fest. I think not, Lucas. I think not.

"You have a tattoo?" Matt asks, curiously smiling while squeezing my inner thigh.

"No, I didn't," I say, looking at Lucas. "Yes, I do," I say with a slight smile to Matt. I'm really trying not to divulge its location at this dinner right now because I don't think anyone's parents want me to explain why Lucas knows I have a very small butterfly right on my panty line. *Only visible if I'm not wearing any panties*.

After desert, Mrs. Atherton directs everyone to the bonfire they had another company set up. It's closer to the water, with luxurious chairs placed neatly around it. At this point in the night, everyone is pretty drunk.

I started slowing down my drinks around dinner only because I've already gotten sick in front of Matt more times than I'd like to count. We all make our way over to the seats as the music starts playing near. Carter grabs Lauren, and they dance around the fire. Mr. and Mrs. Atherton follow suit. Everyone's laughs and smiles are warming to see. This is a celebration, after all. I get up, extending my hand to Matt. He takes my hand in his, and I lead him away from the seat. He spins me around, grabbing my waist and twirling me again. His laughs are deep, like his voice, but not as rough. I like when he laughs. It always makes me involuntarily smile. He brings me close to him and wraps his arm around my waist, kissing the side of my head at the same time. I move my face back to look at him, eye to eye. I want to feel his lips on mine so bad. This is kind of like a fourth date, right? Basically a fifth?

"You look beautiful tonight. Did I tell you that already?" he says, holding my gaze.

"I can't remember." I smile, leaning my lips closer to his, kissing him on his cheek right by the corner of his mouth. I hold my lips there, so close to his that our breaths mix together.

"Do you want to go back to the house?" I ask softly.

"If you do." His voice is just a whisper now.

I release myself from his grasp, grabbing his hand to lead the way.

"I'm feeling a little sick from the ride today," I say to Lauren in a groggy tone, hoping I'm faking sick correctly. She doesn't second guess it and gives me a hug. I congratulate her again and tell her I love her.

Matt and I issue goodbyes to everyone at once as I take his hand again to lead him up our stone path.

He's teased me enough. It's my turn now.

CHAPTER FIFTEEN

While walking up the stairs to the front door, my stomach is circling with those damn butterflies that can't seem to go away. Matt stands close behind me, guiding me lightly with his hand on the small of my back. We enter the home and make our way to the kitchen. The vodka sodas I had at dinner have me feeling *great* but leave my mouth dry with a bitter taste. I grab a glass out of the cupboard and offer to get Matt one as well. I fill them with water before pushing myself to sit on the kitchen island.

"Thank you for coming," I say while bringing the glass of water to my lips.

"Of course, I had a great time. Thank you for inviting me," he says while moving a bit closer in my direction. "What time do we have to get up in the morning?"

"Lauren said they are having a chef make breakfast at their place around eight-thirty, so maybe...seven?"

"We should get to bed soon then, yeah?" he asks while moving towards me, putting himself between my legs that dangle off the island.

I set my water glass down to the right of me and throw my arms around his neck, moving him closer to me. I take my hands and gently rub the back of his head, feeling his hair in between my fingers. "I really appreciate you driving me. Sorry I got sick in your car."

He laughs lightly. "I don't mind at all."

I bring my hands around to rest them on the sides of his face. With me sitting so high up, we're eye-to-eye. I inch closer to his mouth, slowly moving my lips to his cheek, kissing him softly. "I should go take a shower before bed," I whisper into his ear.

He lifts me off the counter, and for a split second, my legs wrap around his waist, I'm not sure if it's his belt buckle I feel between my thighs or if it's *him*. He sets me down, and we move to the bedroom.

I grab the black silk dress from the night before that he insisted I bring and head to the bathroom, slightly leaving the door ajar as I undress. I'm not sure if he can see anything or if he's even looking. He can tease and tantalize me all he wants, but he *will* get a taste of his own medicine.

I look through the crack in the door, but there's nobody staring back. Even so, I undress like I'm being watched, moving dreadfully slow with a slight grin pulling at my mouth.

I hop into the shower, and the hot beads of water scorch my back. I gasp slightly as I wasn't expecting it to be that hot. It feels good after a moment, so I don't adjust it. I take my time in the shower, soaking and washing my body off from the day.

After I finish, I grab a towel that was rolled and resting on a black iron rack. I slip on my nightgown and adjust myself, perking my boobs up as high as they can go with these demi cups barely covering my nipples. I move my hair to the front of my shoulders, the bottom ends dripping wet from the shower. As I step out of the bathroom, opening the door more, I can see Matt putting clothes back in his bag. He has dark gray sweatpants on and no shirt. His back muscles move and contract as he lifts and sets down the heavy bag. He turns around to face me with a smile, bringing a hand to his jaw and running his fingers over his bottom lip.

"Fuck," he mutters.

I smile and walk towards the light switch, shutting it off. The moonlight pours into the bedroom, casting a blue hue throughout.

"Sit," I say to him, pointing to one of the big button chairs in the corner of the room. He looks at me curiously, then does as I ask. I walk towards him and stand directly in front of him, kneeling right between his legs. I can see his breath deepen in his chest as I do this. I place my hands on his knees and slowly glide them up to the tops of his thighs.

"Matt," I say, looking up at him with hungry eyes. "I want to see you come."

His eyes widen as his breaths get deeper. He swallows hard and doesn't move. I take his hand and bring it to my lips, taking his index finger and pushing it inside my mouth to suck on it. As my tongue drags along, he lets out a slight groan. I take his middle finger and do the same, pushing it inside my mouth as I suck, moving from the bottom to the tip of his finger. I move his hand away and place it right on his lap, guiding him over his sweatpants back and forth. I watch him stroke himself.

I sit back on my heels, with my hands on my thighs. His eyes piercing me with every move I make. I slide my hands to the hem of my dress, pulling it up a little bit to expose more skin on my thighs. He sighs, and I see his cock grow beneath his sweatpants.

"Keep going." I let out a heavy breath. I move my legs to the front of me and open them up, bending my knees slightly to expose my matching black thong. He dips his hands inside his sweatpants, pulling out his hard, thick cock. I breathe heavily and smile slightly as I nod, telling him to keep going. He does, and I drag my fingers on my inner thigh, spreading wider to clear his view, then trace my finger around the outside of my panty line. He moves his hand up and down, gripping harder. His breathing gets heavier as he spits in his hand and places it back on himself.

My heart quickens. I can see the way it pulses under his hand, the hand that's barley fitting around it. I want it. I want *him* inside of me. I slowly move my hand up to my neck, drawing it down my skin lightly as I move over my collarbone, then down my chest, until I get to the lace barely covering my nipple. His hand moves faster as I trace the pattern of the lace.

I bring my hand down to my panties and slide my finger underneath, dipping it far inside me. I gasp as I feel my finger go in deep, and I pull it out, bring it to my lips, and taste myself, just like he did. He moans and throws his head back, speeding up the rhythm of his hand. He brings his head back to look at me like he doesn't want to miss a thing. My heart is pounding, and my stomach is in knots. I want him to come, but I want to come too. I slide my finger back under my panties, circling my clit lightly. He spits on his hand again, and I moan. The sight of him spitting sends my heart racing even faster. He slows down his rhythm, focusing on the head of his cock. Seeing him twist his hand around it makes my pussy throb, and I move my panties over to the side, exposing myself to him.

"Fuck." He can hardly get out because his breath is quickening.

I dip my finger back inside me, spreading my wetness over my clit. I circle around it, pressing more firmly, and groan as I tilt my head back. I hear him moan again, and I move faster on myself, bringing my eyes back to meet his. He's stroking his cock, right in the center, vigorously. My jaw drops, and I can feel myself tense. He moans again, and I know he's close. I'm close too.

"I'm gonna come," I whimper.

He opens his mouth as if he's sucking in air. "Fuck," he groans. "Fuck Vivian."

"I'm coming," I cry. My legs shake as I circle my clit faster, and my stomach tenses. I hear him groan harder while I look him in the eyes. He throws his head back as his hot come drips down his knuckles. The sounds of his short breaths and grunting fill my ears. My pussy contracts, sending me in a spiral, and I cry out, moaning harder and moving my hips. His rhythm has stopped, and I slow down. Trying to catch my breath and stop my heart from beating out of my chest. I move my hand away and sigh. Looking at him, I sigh with a light laugh of relief. *Holy fuck*.

He smiles at me, grinning from ear to ear. Our breaths loud, our chests visibly striving for air. *This fucking man*. My heart flutters. Looking at him feels euphoric, and the emotions that wash over me have me feeling like I could cry at any second. I slowly sit up, crossing my legs. I tilt my head up slightly to look at him.

"We should probably get to bed," I say with a smile.

"I agree." He grins.

As he cleans up in the bathroom, I move under the sheets. The high tread count feels cold against my skin, and I settle further into bed as I hear the bathroom light shut off. Matthew walks to the other side, sliding in next to me. His eyes look calm as he smiles, moving his arm over me, bringing my body closer to his. Our faces close as he locks in my gaze, staring at me with his chocolate eyes.

"You're so beautiful," he says softly. I smile as he kisses my forehead. His body heats against mine.

He brings his hand to my face and slightly moves my bangs, running his finger lightly across my scar. I hadn't noticed since then that the scar above his eyebrow is hardly visible; a thin white line is all it appears to be.

"Fate," he whispers.

I tilt my head up to look at his eyes closer, pondering the word he just spoke.

Do I believe in fate? Not really. My father taught me to be a realist. We make our own destinies and such. But even I can't deny this—the coincidence surrounding how we collided and how everything has changed since.

He kisses the beginning of my scar, right near the center of my hairline. I smile as I move my head into the crook of his neck, swinging my arm around his body, locking us in together.

"Goodnight, Vivian."

"Goodnight, Matthew," I say as I kiss his chest directly in front of me. I nudge my head on him to get comfortable, and for a split second, I get the feeling that this is where I am meant to be.

Right here, with him, *for the rest of my life.*

CHAPTER SIXTEEN

I must have dreamt about the accident again. It's not a rare occurrence, but something triggers me to wake in a sweat. The sounds of metal crashing into metal, pelting rain hitting the asphalt, and Matt's voice bringing me to consciousness play repeatedly in my head.

I try to breathe myself calm then glance over at him, sleeping soundly still. Laying back down and forcing my eyes to close is the only thing I can do to make myself fall back asleep, and it seems like time passes in a snap before I feel the sun over my eyes. I open them up slightly to adjust and turn my head over to see Matthew still sleeping. His breath is slow and steady, his lips pursed, and his eyes shut tight. I lean over to kiss him on the cheek softly, then sneak out of bed and head downstairs to start some coffee.

Every drawer in this kitchen is neatly organized, one drawer full of coffee pods, another drawer full of different kinds of tea bags. I grab the first pod I can find that mentions dark roast and pop it in, searching for a coffee mug next. Visions of last night flood my head, Matthew, and the faces he made, the sounds he made, *for me.* I hear his footsteps upstairs as my coffee finishes brewing.

"Want a cup?" I ask him, and his tired eyes catch mine from the stairs.

"Please," he says in a low, gruffer voice than normal.

I smile and turn to open the coffee pod drawer again. There are at least fifteen different kinds, all neatly placed in a row. I have no idea what he likes or what he doesn't like. I stand there for a moment, trying to decide as he comes up right behind me, threading both arms around my waist and peaking over my shoulder.

"Any is fine," he quietly says in my ear as he kisses the side of my head. I grab him a french vanilla because I haven't met anyone who doesn't care for that. It's the *all-black coffee* that I like that I know most people don't.

"Want to sit outside?" he asks as I hand him his cup.

I nod and follow him to the living room, stepping out on the porch through the large french doors. We sit on the two loungers facing the ocean soaking up the weather. It's a little breezy by the water, but not too cold. At least

Matt put a shirt on. I'm still in a barley there dress with the smallest straps on the planet. After some silence, he asks, "So you went to school for business, huh? Why business? Why Boston?"

"Business was what my guidance counselor suggested, I had no idea, so I just went with it. And why Boston? I don't know..my parents visited there a lot, and I figured there must have been something special about it, or they wouldn't have kept coming back. Around the time my dad died, I was just starting to fill out college applications. I didn't really have a plan. My dad took my mom's entire life insurance and kept it in savings for college for me. I felt like I *had* to go. So I did."

"Good for you," Matt says, taking a sip from his mug. "How old were you again? When your parents died?"

"I was twelve when my mom passed and seventeen when my dad did," I say, looking down at the black coffee in my cup. It feels strange to talk about this with him, even with how intimate we just were last night.

My face must show my slight discomfort because he's quick to ask, "Do you have a lot of good memories with them?"

I'm not sure if he's looking at me like this because he's sorry for my loss, or he's sorry for his own. I perk up at his question. "Tons. They were the best parents. But I lost them both when my Mom died...my dad was never the same."

"That can happen when you lose someone you love."

Again, it feels so strange. Maybe because I am used to keeping my family a secret. My own personal tragedy that I bury and try not to use to get me ahead in the world. I don't want sympathy or handouts. I don't want anyone looking at me differently.

I am not lost. I just lost people.

And I don't want to hurt Matthew by gloating about my childhood. I mean, how fucked up that both of my parents being dead before I turned eighteen is gloating to someone. That should be like the worst-case scenario. He smiles at me, though, then takes my hand in his, squeezing lightly. We both look back at the sea and remain quiet. I take a deep breath, and the smells fill my nose – coffee with a pinch of salt.

"What do you think they'll have for breakfast?" I ask, breaking the silence, ready to change the topic. And, well, my stomach is turning.

"Something good, I hope." He laughs. "Should we get ready?"

I nod, and we stand up. He takes my hand in his, intertwining our fingers. I follow him back into the house and up to the bedroom.

"We're leaving right after breakfast, right?" I ask, turning my head back to him, then lift my nightgown over my head.

"Yes, that's fine," he says with a deep voice.

I can feel his eyes on me. I had forgotten he hasn't seen much of my body, and right now, he has a perfect view of my bare back and ass. I slip over my black sports bra and matching biker shorts and turn around to face him. He hasn't moved a muscle, still standing there staring at me with his shirt in his hands. He flashes a smile and then pulls the shirt over his head before he drops his sweatpants and puts on jeans, walking towards me as he buttons them. Standing close to me, he lifts his hands to my cheeks and brings my face closer to his.

"Just so you know, after our fifth date, nothing will stop me from kissing you on the lips every second of every day." He brushes my bottom lip with his thumb and kisses me on the tip of my nose.

My heart pounds, and I swear I can hear the beat of it in my eardrums. All I can do at this moment is stand here, smiling from ear to ear, looking at him with lust, or love. I can't tell the difference between the two at this point. All I know is he's magnetic...and I'm just a pile of fucking metal.

We lock up the house following the instructions in my email and walk next door to where Lauren and Carter are staying. The house is at least three times the size of the one we stayed in. Grey in color, more modern feel to the outside than ours. We walk into a grand foyer. Stairs lead up to the next level from both sides. Only the living room is visible from where we are standing.

"Good morning!" Lauren shouts.

"Good morning," I fire back, following her voice.

We make our way into the living room, seeing the kitchen and dining are to the left.

"You guys sit right here. They are almost finished with breakfast," she says while pulling out a chair from the large dining table filled with floral arrangements.

We take a seat as Lauren's dad strikes up his previous conversation with Matt from the night before. Mr. Atherton seems to be taking kindly to Matt, learning about his job, his schooling, you name it.

"So…it's going well?" Lauren whispers in my ear next to me.

"I can't wait to tell you everything. Holy fuck Lauren." I match her tone, only more excited.

"Jesus, Viv, spill the beans."

"Lo, I can't." I chuckle.

"Vivian Elizabeth Westwood, you better tell me right now," she demands quietly with a smile.

"I, uh, I saw it," I say, trying to be as quiet as possible.

"Huh?"

"I saw....*it*."

"His...?" She gasps.

"Breakfast is served," a chef says from behind the long dark grey island. Sprawled out buffet style is quite possibly every breakfast food you could imagine.

Everyone starts to stand up as Lauren and I try to wait it out so I can tell her more.

"I'll get you a plate," Matt says as he moves behind my chair, placing his hands on my shoulders and bending down to kiss the top of my head. Lauren's mouth drops as her eyes stay fixed on Matt.

"He's getting you a plate? Oh, you guys definitely fucked. Carter won't even get *me* a plate."

"No, not yet. I told him we had to wait five dates."

"Five dates? Why? Since when? Vivian, you've never waited for sex in your life...please," she scoffs jokingly.

"Exactly," I reply. "He's just different. I wanted to take it slow. I feel I rush everything, Lo. He's just too good. I didn't want to ruin it."

"So how did you see his...uh.."

I just smile, biting my lower lip.

"If you don't call me the second you're home and tell me every last detail, I will be thoroughly pissed off at you for at least a day. Do you hear me?" Her face takes on her usual stern, non-nonsense act. Then her voice drops to a whisper, "Just tell me...was it big?"

I purse my lips in a tight smile while Matt returns, placing my plate in front of me.

"*And thick,*" I say, leaning over to get closer to her.

She lets out one loud laugh as she slams her hand on the table, forcing everyone's attention on her.

With a little embarrassment, she clears her throat and says, "I should, uh...get some food."

"Thank you, Matt." I look over at him.

"I didn't know what you would like, so I kind of got you everything."

"I appreciate it." I lean to my left and kiss his cheek. He wasn't kidding; he did get me everything. A scone, scrambled eggs, hash browns, American fries, fruit, bacon, sausage, and a waffle. I like to eat, but this plate is stacked a little too high for my stomach.

As we start on breakfast, Carter and Lauren's family reminisce about the two as children. I love hearing stories about Lauren when she was little, but it's nice to hear more about Carter too. It's been a great conversation, and it certainly helps that Lucas is still in bed. Apparently, he was too drunk last night and is utterly sick this morning. *Poor thing*.

"So Vivian, how long have you and Matt been together?" Mrs. Atherton asks, directing the table's focus to us.

I gulp as I swallow the orange juice already in my mouth before she even asked. I don't know what to say. We're *not* together? I don't know what the hell we are even doing, but I know what we are *not* doing.

"We've known each other a couple of months." Matt swings his arm around my shoulder.

I grin, taking a breath and placing my hand on his leg, giving him a little squeeze as a thank you.

"How wonderful. New love is always so exciting," she states, smiling from ear to ear.

I grin back nervously, panicking in silence. I can't even look at Matt right now I'm so embarrassed. *Love?* Jesus. I can't appear any more uncomfortable than Lauren, though. She seems mortified while looking at her mother.

"Ok, mom! We should start packing," Lauren announces.

We have finished breakfast but spent at least another thirty minutes just chatting. It is time to go, though, Matt will have to be back to work later tonight, and I have to work early in the morning tomorrow. We all get up, saying our goodbyes, giving our hugs and handshakes. Matt walks me out the door, guiding me with that hand of his on the small of my back.

"I stole a plastic bag from our house," he says, pulling a small grocery bag out from his jean pocket. "In case you get sick."

"Thank you." I grab the bag from him and smile. As embarrassed as I want to be right now, I can't. *How thoughtful of him.*

CHAPTER SEVENTEEN

"**Y**ou masturbated with him?!" Lauren shouts across our very small table to me.

"We still need another minute," I say to the waiter who so inconveniently arrived.

I feel the embarrassment heating my cheeks. "Lauren!" I laugh through it. "Keep your voice down! We're in public, for fucks sake."

Since Lauren was coming home from Montauk only three days after me, I wanted to tell her in person. Hindsight is twenty-twenty, though, since now everyone at dinner knows I got myself off with a man I haven't even had sex with yet.

Lauren, entirely unmoved by the gawking neighboring tables, gives me a look that borders impressed. "I don't know if I could have done it. How could you *not* just fuck him right then and there?"

"It was hard." I giggle. "In more ways than one."

We laugh loudly. God, I missed her being home.

"So this is all after you puked in his car, correct?"

"Yes..." I say, grinding my teeth. "I would like to forget about that one. But, on the bright side, we made it all the way home without any incidents."

"Good for you. I'm so proud." She brings her glass to mine, clinking them together in a cheers. "Have you heard from him since?"

"Kind of, he went to work right when we got back, and he's working all week, so I'm not really sure when I'll see him next."

"So this next date...this is it, right?" she says as her eyebrows perk up.

"Yeah, but he's got to ask me about it first." I laugh, masking my nervousness.

The truth is, I *haven't* really talked to him at all. It's only been three days, but after the time we spent together over the weekend, I guess I was at least expecting a quick 'hello' at some point. I actually don't know when his next day off is or if he plans to spend the day with me. Of course, yesterday at work, when I was stocking the shelves, all I could think about was if I somehow upset him in

Montauk. I don't think I did at all, but my mind can't help but replay every little scenario to think of why he hasn't bothered to at least text me.

"Are you okay?" Lauren asks as the waiter brings our food to the table.

"Yeah, I'm good. I...I just..." I fumble over my words, trying to think of the perfect lie, only coming up with the truth instead. "I haven't talked to Matt... at all. He hasn't texted or called or..showed up or anything. Tomorrow will be *four* days, Lauren. Doesn't that seem like a long time?"

She sits there, soaking in my words. Stunned or shocked, I'm not sure.

"Four days?" she repeats the two words.

I nod. "I mean, I thought we had a great time. Maybe it's because I won't fuck him yet — I don't know, I just feel...I just feel like if he wanted to hear from me, he would have reached out. Maybe I'm overthinking it but," I ramble on, not being able to finish my thought before the waiter reappears.

"Can I get you," The waiter interrupts.

"Can you get her another drink, please?" Lauren responds quickly. "Honey, what are you doing tonight?

"Nothing, I-" I try to spit out before she interrupts *me* this time.

"The Collins and Ash Firm is having a celebration party tonight. They just won a huge case. Please come with me," she says.

I don't know if this is a *I feel sorry for you* invite to Carter's law firm get-together or not, but I didn't have any plans tonight besides wallowing in my self-pity, so this seems like a better option.

"What should I wear?" I smile, still unsure, but maybe I can get shit-faced and just forget about Matt not reaching out, at least for one night.

"Just come to my house after dinner. I have the perfect dress for you."

Lauren and I finish eating and get a ride service back to her place. Thankfully, she and Carter's apartment is only eight blocks from here, and the party is at Ezra Ash's penthouse, which is the building next to theirs. At least I won't be car sick on Lauren's rather expensive gown she's about to put me in.

"This is...this is something Lo," I say, looking over my shoulder in her closet mirror.

"You look fab, don't stress."

"What if I ruin it?" I mutter. I don't do well in white. Lauren should know this.

"Oh well, it doesn't fit me as well as it fits you anyways," she says, throwing her hand at me while rifling through her racks to find me matching shoes. "Do you not like it?" She stops, standing straight and looking at me with curious eyes.

"No, I love it. Just, are you sure it looks good on me?" I ask as I lay my hands flatly over the sleek fit of the gown running down my body.

"Oh, shut up, Viv! You look stunning. You're the only person I know who can pull off a backless dress."

I have to admit, it does look stunning. The white gown is rimmed with pearls on the edges, complimenting my olive skin. Tiny pearls crisscross the upper part of my shoulders in the back. Other than that, the gown is completely bare behind, falling right above my bottom.

"You girls about ready?" Carter calls from outside of the bedroom.

"Uh, just a minute!" Lauren calls out to him as she throws a shirt to the floor.

"I can't find these damn shoes!" she grunts.

"What about these?" I hold up a pair of white satin kitten heels.

"Those are it! Put them on. Let's get drunk," she says with a mischievous smile. "Oh, Carter! We're ready!"

She already may be feeling a buzz. I did see her suck down four Chardonnays at dinner. We both socially drink. I think we have fed off each other that way. A party, an event, or any kind of social setting where we may be forced into small chit-chat or meeting new people, we need a drink. I'm sure there are better coping mechanisms for social anxiety, but unfortunately, neither one of us has found that yet, but I'm sure we will let the other one know when we do.

As we walk out the front door to their apartment building, I check my phone once more for any new messages. Besides my twenty percent battery notification, I've got nothing. I shove my phone into the clutch Lauren let me borrow and brush the hair out of my eyes as we walk to the building next door. The doorman lets us in with a wave.

As we make our way to the elevators, Carter pushes the PH button. I've never actually been in a penthouse before, but I've seen it in movies. Some look grand. Others look too bland for the penthouse price tag. Judging by the chandeliers and the armed security in the lobby, I would say this will probably be one of the more grand penthouses. The elevator dings and we step out.

Two words. *Boston. Skyline.*

I have simply never seen anything like this before. I can't see how someone could wake up to this view every day and be unhappy. It just doesn't seem possible. The home itself is gorgeous on its own with an open floor concept, and don't even get me started on the staff walking around with trays of champagne.

"Thank you!" I say as I pluck off the fullest glass from the platter and glance at the liquid. Here's to forgetting about Matt. *Drink one.*

We make our way closer inside, finding Carter's partner Ezra. I've only met him once when he was married to his former wife...I forgot her name, but she seemed like a bitch. Ezra seems quite older than me, maybe in his early thirties. Definitely easy to look at. The portion of salt and pepper that runs through the sides of his hair serves him well.

"Hello, Ladies." Ezra nods at Lauren and me. "You both look exquisite."

We smile as Carter talks to him about their last court case.

"Want to find some snacks?" Lauren whispers close to my face.

"I thought you'd never ask," I mumble back into her ear.

We leave the little circle Ezra and Carter made with us and look towards the kitchen to see if they have any appetizers.

Nothing.

"Lo, open a cupboard or something and see if there are some chips," I joke.

She laughs, then snorts. Oh yeah, she's toasted.

"Let me tell Carter to ask Ezra for some snacks," she whispers.

I'm not sure why she's being quiet. It's decently loud in here with the light jazz music playing behind the voices of at least thirty grown adults mingling. She scoots past the counter and finds Carter in the crowd. I stand still, sipping on my champagne. It's the fancy kind, too, I know I'm going to have a raging headache in the morning.

"So you're looking for food, huh?" a thick voice says from behind. I spin around to see Ezra, standing there in his couple thousand dollar worth suit and his Rolex that costs more than my rent for a whole year. He *looks* arrogant, although I have no idea if he truly is or not.

"Did Lauren rat on me?" I laugh.

He chuckles. "She did, but I came over to let you know I've got some appetizers coming out in a bit, or I can find a granola bar in the pantry for you."

I give him a grin. The wait staff comes around with more glasses of champagne lined around the platter. Ezra grabs two and hands me one, taking the near-empty glass out of my hands before disposing of it back on the tray.

"Thank you, and as long as you have food coming, I'll be patient," I say with soft eyes.

He takes a step back, biting his lip softly and nodding his head, looking me up and down. "You wear that dress well." His lips pinch at a sly grin.

What the fuck. My heart speeds up, and my body instantly warms as I look around the room for Lauren. I take a large sip and lean my back on the counter. It's cold against my fevered skin.

"Thank you," I say with a reserved grin. "You don't look so bad yourself," I continue, the champagne setting in as my cheeks run hotter. I see Lauren and politely excuse myself before I head straight to her, nudging my way into the circle she is in with Carter and a couple of colleagues.

"Did you get us a snack?" she asks me.

"*Bitch*, you were supposed to be asking for the snacks, not ratting me out." I laugh with a wide smile, teasing her lovingly. We stand and listen to the men use legal jargon, none of which she or I know. We're just happy to be sucking down the free drinks they keep replenishing.

"Where are those fucking appetizers?" Lauren groans in my ear; it's been at least twenty minutes. I look around, trying to find any waitstaff around.

"Hold on," I move past her and head towards the kitchen, spotting Ezra. "Maybe I will take that granola bar." I walk up, placing my hand on his elbow.

He grins, making the lines on his face more prominent. "Follow me."

I walk behind him through the large kitchen to a door off to the side. He opens it to reveal an oversized pantry. Cereal is in containers. Pasta is in containers. Why is everything in containers and not in the fucking boxes? It's aesthetically pleasing, I'll give him that, but Christ, is it really worth all the work?

"Here you go," he says as he hands me the chocolate chip granola bar. I grab it, but he doesn't let go.

"Thank you," I say, looking up into his inviting emerald eyes.

"Do you need anything else?" He asks, still holding onto the bar. I can smell his cologne as he moves a step closer to me. My nose fills with oakmoss and bergamot, and I slightly tug on my bottom lip instinctively.

"I think that's it," I say, locking in his eyes, flashing a smile to show my teeth.

"Vivian, right?" he asks, brushing my bottom lip lightly with his thumb.

I nod to his question before he draws my bottom lip down, wrapping his other arm around my waist and pulling my torso to his.

I glance at his lips. They look soft. His face is clean-shaven, and everything just looks smooth. "You really shouldn't bite that lip around me," he says with sinister grin. "But I'm glad you're here, Vivian." He breathes onto my lips as his forehead rests on mine. He lets go of the granola bar and brings that hand to my cheek, gripping me and pulling me in. His lips crush on mine, and his tongue dives in for a taste.

I sweep my tongue with his as our lips press together. He removes the hand around my waist and brings it to my other cheek, grabbing my face with both hands. We move our lips together as he goes back in, rushing his tongue into my mouth. I whimper as he bites my bottom lip softly.

What the fuck?

What the fuck am I doing?

I have to stop. What would Matt think?

Oh my god, *Matt*.

I break his force away, removing my mouth with his and taking a quick step back.

"I'm sorry, I — I have to go," I say as I turn around and push the pantry door open. I burst out into the kitchen and spot Lauren, moving quickly to her.

"Here, I have to go. I'll call you later." I hand her the granola bar and exit the room, hastily pushing the elevator button. *Shit.* What did I just do? I'm fine, it's fine. Matt and I aren't even a thing. We're not official. He hasn't talked to me in three days. *Three days.* **No**...Four days. It's after midnight. How does he think that makes me feel?

I jog out the front door. Stopping on the street to look around.

Where the fuck am I?

My sense of direction is shot with all of the champagne I've had tonight, and Lauren just moved into Carter's apartment next door not too long ago. I've only been here a handful of times and haven't walked the route yet.

I type in my home address, which is thirty-eight minutes to walk. Okay, it's fine. I'm in kitten heels, basically flats. Jesus Christ, what did I do? You know, one could argue this is Matt's fault. Really, who gets off for someone and then doesn't have the decency to call? I mean, besides me, every other hook-up, but that's not the point here.

Yeah, fuck him.

I start to walk, reminding myself it's one foot in front of the other. Occasionally I sway to the side, but I would blame the wind for that one. As I get further from the penthouse, my anger builds up. I have to say something — I've never been one to be known for keeping my mouth shut.

Me: why have t you called yrt

I can't type and walk, and I certainly can't type when I'm drunk.

I can't call a ride service, I have one percent battery left on my phone, and I've never walked this late in Boston by myself before, especially wearing a gown and heels. It's not terrible, except for the dark parts of a street where I swear I hear someone whistling at me, but that's okay — full steam ahead.

Matthew: Are you drunk? Where are you?

Don't worry. I was just making out with some guy in a pantry, no problem.

Yeah, I can't tell him that. Or maybe I should. I don't get another chance to think about it before my phone dies, and I throw it back in my clutch. Someone whistles at me again, and I look around, nearly stopping in my tracks to try and see through the dim lighting of the street lamps.

I don't have a weapon, *but I've got a heel*. I could quickly kick my foot up to get it off and then attack whoever was attacking me with it, right? Maybe I should try first so that way I'm prepared.

Let's just....

Kick it up...

and I just broke the heel.

Oh, great. Ok, so I'm down one shoe. Not a big deal. I'm at least coming up to an overpass, I think, so there are no other houses or people, just really fast cars.

As I walk, I should say limp, with one heel on and the other kitten heel in my hand, I spot a car from the corner of my eye starting to slow down. *Shit.* I'm going to get kidnapped, or killed, or even worse, kidnapped than killed. Before I can think of any other scenarios in my head, the car pulls next to me and rolls down the passenger window.

"Matt?!" I shout as I stop dead in my tracks. "What are you doing here?"

"Get in," he snaps.

I don't argue with him. My feet hurt, and all I want to do is go home. I open the passenger door and get in, only noticing for a moment that he's in dark blue scrubs and the stubble on his face is more prominent.

"Where were you?" he asks.

"At a party," I say, still facing forward with one heel in my hand. "Why did you come to get me?"

"I knew you were drinking. I tried to call you, but it went straight to voicemail, so I texted Carter to see if he knew where you were. I saw how far away it was from your house, and I did not want you to walk it alone at night, so I was just driving your route until I could find you."

"Did you leave work to get me?" I ask softly.

"I just got off. I've been at the hospital since we got back. I have to go back in the morning, but at least I can sleep in my own bed tonight," he breathes.

"Why haven't you called me?" I mutter after some silence.

"Why haven't I what?" he asks curiously, probably not hearing a word that I just said.

"I kissed someone tonight."

"You what?" he asks, his tone growing more fierce.

I still haven't looked at his face to read his expressions.

"He kissed me, and then I stopped it. Well, I kissed him back, and *then* I stopped it." My head involuntarily turns to him, trying to explain. I see his face. He looks tired and worn down. The veins in his hand pop out from him, gripping the steering wheel so hard.

"Can you explain one thing to me — please?" he asks through gritted teeth, but I can tell he's trying to stay calm.

"How is it that I have to wait before I can kiss you, and you can meet some fucking prick anywhere, and rules don't apply to him?"

The answer slips out without pause. "He doesn't mean anything to me."

"And that makes it okay?"

"No, Matt. I....why haven't you called or texted me at least?" My eyes start to become glossy.

"What do you mean, Viv?" he questions as we come to a stop on my street. He pulls into a parking space and shuts the car off, shifting his body directly toward me. "Look at me," he demands softly.

"Since we've been home, you haven't reached out...I just want to know why? Did I do something?" I whimper, trying to hold back tears. I have no idea why my eyes are welling with water. It's probably the drinks getting to me. I hardly ever cry anymore.

"Vivian, listen to me. I work *a lot*." He takes a deep breath, collecting himself. "I haven't had a real girlfriend in years. I've dated here and there, but nothing ever lasted."

"Nothing has lasted for me, either," I counter. "But texting isn't hard."

"I'm sorry, Vivian. I had no idea you would be upset about that. I was going to call you after work tomorrow to see if you were free. Had I known, I would have called you every single chance I got some form of a break. I promise I'll do better," he says as his eyes soften.

"I'm sorry I kissed him," I say back, bringing my hands to my face and covering myself. He lowers my hands gently as a tear falls from my right eye. He wipes it away with his thumb and caresses my cheek.

"It just happened, and as soon as I realized, I pushed him off and left. That's why I was walking home. I'm sorry. It didn't mean anything. I don't care about him. I care about *you*."

The funny thing about drinking is that whatever truths are living inside you tend to come out a lot easier when alcohol is involved.

"I only want you, Matt. I thought you didn't want me. I just made a mistake."

Matt nods. "Can we both agree not to make impulsive choices when we're upset with each other?"

"Deal."

He wraps this hand to the back of my neck, threading my tresses between his fingers, and brings his face closer to mine. The tips of our top lips almost touch, and a surge of electricity flows between us. "Please don't kiss anyone else but me, Vivian," he whispers onto my lips. "I'll call you tomorrow and every day after. Okay?"

I nod slightly as my heart pounds faster. His breath dances on my mouth. I close my lips together, which makes them brush slightly against his. He kisses me on the cheek gently. "Do you want me to walk you up?"

"Not tonight. Go get some sleep. Thank you...for taking me home," I say in a hushed tone before stepping out of his car.

I shut the door and take in a deep breath—my pulse beating at rapid fire. I walk to my door and head straight upstairs—ready for this night to be done with. I'm happy, confused, and *oh so drunk*.

CHAPTER EIGHTEEN

The line to Birch Books is out of the door. Literally. Bill says this place has never been this busy before. Alana Debose is doing her book signing here in two weeks, but she has been raving about the place on her social media, which I'm assuming, is where all the traffic is coming from today. This place isn't *big* by any means, so a line of ten plus waiting to get in is huge for us. I stay behind the counter, cashing out customers as most of them buy Alana's newest book. Caroline is in the back ordering more inventory as it evaporates, and Bill...Bill is still sick, but he's in the back too. I've already tried to take him home once, but if looks could kill, I would have been blown to bits with the look he shot me after I suggested that.

I haven't read any of Alana's books, it's not the typical genre I like, but with the number of people here today, she must be a damn good writer to have some kind of following like that.

My phone buzzes next to me on the counter as I'm ringing up a customer. I glance at it as it lights up.

Matthew: Good morning. Are you free tonight?

I feel terrible about last night. I made him out to be some sort of jackass. After everything that's happened between us so far, after some of the things he's said to me, the way he looks at me...how could I think he wasn't being genuine. I know he's a doctor, and if I didn't have my head shoved so far up my ass, I would have naturally known he would be busy. And I don't want to come off as needy either, which is exactly what I did. I should be thankful he even wants to continue seeing me, honestly. I want to reply to him, but there's no way I'm going to have a chance to pull out my phone anytime soon. This place is packed.

"Go home, Bill, get some rest," I demand jokingly as he emerges from the curtain, placing last month's figure sheets next to me on the counter.

"I'll rest when I'm dead," he grunts, waving his hand at me to shoo me off as he heads back to his office.

"That'll be eighteen dollars and fifty cents," I say to the tall blonde customer. My phone buzzes again. And again. And again.

Matthew: Are
Matthew: You
Matthew: Free
Matthew: Tonight

I smirk at the customer, trying to break the awkwardness of my phone breaking the silence between us. She hands me her cash, and I toss my phone in my purse on the floor, continuing with the rest of the line. A line that lasted a little over an hour. We had to have made over a thousand dollars during that rush. Once everyone has left, I run into the back to tell Bill and Caroline. We're all giddy like kids on Christmas.

"Why don't you lock it up at five, and let's all play a game of cards? Then you can go, Vivy. How about that?" Bill says, grinning so large his eyes squint.

"Are you sure you want to close an hour early? We can still play cards after."

"Nope. Lock it up, doll. I gotta kick your girls' ass in some poker." He slaps his hands together, a smile plastered on his face.

"Bill, don't get smart now. Remember who cooks your meals for ya," Caroline snaps with a wink.

I stand there and laugh, agreeing to lock up at five o'clock per his request. I go back to the front to find only one person browsing the shelves. I grab my phone and text Matt back.

Me: Sorry! Busy day. I'm free later. At the store until 6:00 maybe.

As five o'clock rolls around, I start to clean up from the day. Wiping down the two end tables near the door and shutting the table lamp off. Straightening up the books on the other large table and putting any loose ones that may be on the chairs back in the bookshelves. After the front looks perfect, I lock the door and push through the curtain to go to Bill's office. My phone buzzes in my hand.

Matthew: I'll be there to pick you up at 6

He's going to pick me up? *Shit.* I was hoping I would have worn something different for our next date rather than ripped jeans and a gray long-sleeve.

"You ready?" Bill asks as he sits behind his desk, shuffling the cards with the lamp light on.

"You're going down, Bill," I say matter-of-factly.

Truth is. I have no fucking clue how to play poker.

I sit next to Caroline on the other side of his desk. Bill deals out the cards and throws us some fake chips to play with, along with three chips in the middle.

"Caroline," I whisper out of the corner of my mouth to her. She looks at me. "What do I do?" I show her my five cards.

"Call," she whispers back.

Call? What the fuck does that mean?

I look at my chips and look back at Caroline, shrugging my shoulders. "Put a chip in," she says faintly.

I do as she says, then she goes next.

"Fold," Bill puts his cards face down.

I see he didn't add any more money, so that must mean he's out. I glance at Caroline as she discards two of her cards. She grabs my hand to see mine again and takes three out. Bill gives me a new set of three and her a new set of two. *Ok*. I think we can manage. I don't know why I just don't ask for some help. I'm sure they would show me. But Bill loves to play. I don't want to waste his time trying to teach me.

Let's play cards.

After forty minutes of *Call, Fold, and Raise*. I think I'm getting the hang of it. The only problem is I'm not sure how they determine the winner. I had a pair once, but Caroline had a bunch of numbers. They got excited, and she won that pot. I'm sure I'll catch on next time. I'm out of chips, and Bill is all in. Caroline has all that she won stacked neatly in front of her.

"Fold," Bill says with a smile.

"I told you, Bill, I told you," Caroline says, laughing as she sweeps the chips from the middle onto her side.

"Oh well, the kids got to get going to catch the sunset anyways," Bill says as he cleans the cards up.

"Huh?" I say lightly.

"Bill, Matty said it was a surprise. Hush your mouth," Caroline snaps.

I grin and laugh as Bill grinds his teeth and widens his eyes.

"Oopsies," he says quietly. "Go ahead, Vivy. We'll lock it up." He smirks after we all hear a knock coming from the front door.

I smile and say goodbye as I walk towards the door and grab my purse before I unlock it.

"Matt." I smile.

"You ready?" He grins.

I nod in return.

"Goodbye!" I shout over my shoulder to Bill and Caroline before I shut the front door. Matt takes my hand with his, interlocking our fingers. I turn my head and look up at him, and I can't help but smile. "So where are we going?" I ask him.

"Well, I thought we could watch the sunset. Does that sound okay?" he says with a soft expression and a deep tone.

I smile, my face flushed, and my eyes flamed with desire. "I don't care where we go, Matt. As long as I'm with you."

CHAPTER NINETEEN

The sky is swirled with strikes of bright orange, cream-colored clouds, and hints of wisteria. The first time I saw that shade of purple in the sky was the morning my mother died. Ever since then, every time I see it, I feel like it's her way of saying she's with me.

I take a moment to think about her more deeply – her smile, the way she laughed. Her ability to see the positive in situations where there was very little. All the little details I've come to miss over the years.

We get out of the car, and Matt walks to the trunk, opens it, and takes out a large white blanket and a wicker basket. I stand to the side, smiling at him, wondering how in the world he had time to plan this. I've never had a picnic before. Not on a beach, not in a park. Another thing I've only seen in the movies.

"You ready?" He grins. I follow him onto the sidewalk, finding a spot in the grass under a tree overlooking the water where the boats line the docks. "We still have about thirty minutes until the sun sets, so I figured we could have some dinner." He says with a closed mouth smile.

We find a spot in the grass, and I help him lay the blanket out. He sets the basket on top, and I sit next to him. He kisses the side of my head before reaching for the basket and pulling out our spread for the night.

"I know you like sushi, but I didn't know what kind, so I got a couple of ones for you," he says with a big smile while laying everything out in front of us. "A bottle of wine for you and a bottle of water for me." He laughs. "I also packed us some fruit and these macarons I grabbed from the bakery by my house... I hope you like this stuff."

My breath catches in my throat as I look at him. His eyes are kind and calm. A wave of warmth washes over me. I nearly shake my head in disbelief. Disbelief that anything like this could ever happen to me.

"It's perfect!" I lean over and kiss him on the cheek. "Thank you." I hold his stare for only a moment before I open up the bottle of wine with the corkscrew he put in the basket. He really thought of everything. There's even two linen hand towels in here, striped and tan colored. I pour the wine into a glass as he pours the water into his.

"To more sunsets with you," he says as he clinks his glass with mine. My stomach swirls as I take a sip. We lean in and open up the food.

"So work was busy, huh? Truthfully? Or Caroline's version of busy?" Matt chuckles.

"Actually busy." I nod and smile. "Literally a line out of the door. How was work for you? Save any lives today?"

"A few, actually." He smirks as he leans in. "I'm off tomorrow too. Got any plans?"

"I'll be at the store until five." I press my lips with a curl.

We eat as he tells me about the last couple of nights at the hospital. I love listening to him talk about his work. He's so passionate and knowledgeable. It amazes me the way he speaks so confidently too. As the sun sets, I shift my body closer, resting my legs on his. He moves his arm around my waist to tuck me into him, and I can feel the warmth of his skin on mine.

"Wisteria," I say quietly. Matt looks down at me with curiosity in his eyes. I look at him, then glance back at the sky, pointing up. "That purple color. Every time I see it, it means my mom is here. At least, to me, it does."

We sit in silence for a moment before he asks, "What was she like?"

"She was..*the best*. She had this way about her. Every time she walked into a room, she grabbed attention. She loved to host parties, and when she did, she could never sit down. She was always up, making sure everyone who came was paid attention to, and acknowledged in some way. She never wanted anyone to feel left out."

I pause only for a moment, I love talking about her, but in the back of my mind, I understand Matt and his brother never had any of this, not even for a second. I can't help but feel sadness for him at the same time.

"Go on," Matt urges me with a smile. "Tell me more."

"She was a great cook. She would cook me breakfast every morning before school and pack my lunches every day, always leaving a note. Those are just a few of my favorite examples. She was a *really great mom*. She would read me a story every night too, sometimes sing a song if I asked." Tears pool in my eyes. Talking about her like this only floods my mind with happy memories, no cloudy judgment over *how* she died.

"You don't talk about your brother much. What is he like?" I say back to him.

"My brother? Well, my brother growing up, was always rowdy. He would always play rough with me, too, probably because I was a lot smaller than him when we were kids." He laughs while dropping his eyes down. "He uh.. wasn't a very good influence..to me..or anyone else for that matter." *He clears his throat.* "I lost contact with him when I was sixteen."

"I'm sorry…" I say softly.

"No." He shakes his head. "It was my choice."

I look up at him. His eyes still dropped to his lap. I place my hand on his leg as he finishes.

"It was ten years since we had spoken when I was around two weeks into my residency at the hospital. We got a call of a possible overdose coming in, and when they brought him in on the stretcher, I knew it was my brother before I stepped any closer."

I suck in air, observing him, his eyes still remaining calm.

"I'm so sorry, Matt, I can't imagine…" I trail off. He doesn't seem distraught talking about it, but I'm sure something like that could weigh heavily on someone's mind. We look back at the sky, holding each other, sitting in silence until he kisses the top of my head.

"This is truly breathtaking," I say as my eyes gleam with the color of the sunset.

"I agree." He smiles. Although his eyes are not on the sky, they are on me.

As the sun further sets, wisteria is gone, and sharp oranges take over, turning into the deepest rust.

"Thank you for all of this tonight," I say looking at him, our eyes locked into each other. Mine bursting with desire, and his with passion.

He smiles as he threads his fingers around my neck to the back of my hair, lightly pulling my face closer to his. He drags his eyes down the length of my face, locking them on my mouth. His lips brush against mine softly, teasing me while only the tips of our lips touch and our breaths collide. I squeeze his leg gently, and he leans in further. Our mouths clash together as he slightly dips his tongue into me. His mouth is hot, and his tongue is soft, caressing mine with every kiss. He tugs my hair softly as he pushes my body slowly down on the blanket, keeping my lips locked with his. He leans over me, with my head on the ground, taking me in his mouth.

I moan slightly as his tongue dips again, further and with more force. His fingers gently sweep above the waist of my jeans, and I whimper quietly into his mouth at the tickling sensation. Pushing my tongue against his, I raise my hand to meet his face and grab onto the back of his head, intertwining my fingers with his soft hair. I grab and pull lightly, shifting his head to the side so I can dive my tongue back into his mouth. He pulls away slightly so we can catch our breaths. We both smile quickly before he dives back in, tugging on my bottom lip and tracing his tongue softly against it. The feeling of his light touch on my lips sends heat to my belly, sweeping the feeling between my legs and thighs. I wrap my lips around his, as his tongue rolls into mine again. He bites on my bottom lip with pressure, our movements becoming more aggressive, and I pull back quickly.

"Take me home," I say with heated eyes. He grins as his eyes gleam. I know he's already playing through all the things he wants to do to me – and I'll gladly let him.

He pulls me up slightly, letting me sit up the rest of the way, and we put all of our food back into the basket before he folds up the blanket. I hook my arm with his as we walk off the grass and onto the walkway, back to the car. He opens the trunk to put everything in, then closes it, grabbing my waist and pushing me gently against the car door. He brings his hands up to my face, cupping my jaw as his thumb brushes my bottom lip, and he leans his face in, possessing my mouth with his gently.

"Vivian, I swear to god I'm going to kiss you for the rest of my life." He breathes into my mouth, and I smile as I kiss him back.

I can't think of anything else this car ride. No accident, no car sickness. I can't close my eyes. I can't close them because they are fixated on *him*. Suddenly, my days seem incomplete without him, my nights ruined without him.

I need him everywhere, all of the time. I stare at him as he drives, and he glances at me occasionally with a smile. At red lights or stop signs, he leans over to plant a kiss on me. I leave it easily accessible by just keeping my head facing him, my lips ready for his. As he parks, my stomach flutters and fills with a rolling heat while my pulse quickens and my breaths become shorter.

"Can I walk you to your door?" he asks, smiling mischievously.

He already knows the answer.

CHAPTER TWENTY

I can hardly get my key in the lock with the anticipation rising inside of me. As soon as I push my front door open, Matt's mouth is back on mine. Kissing me backward into the threshold of my house. We stand in my living room, my arms thrown around his neck. Our heads move side to side, fitting perfectly with one another as our lips crash and collide and our tongues roll together. He kicks my door shut with his foot while keeping his mouth on mine. He grabs the back of my thighs and lifts me up, wrapping my legs around his waist, so our jeans rub together. He swirls his tongue in my mouth before pulling his head back slightly. His breathing short and loud.

"Upstairs?" he sighs heavily.

I nod, and he walks up my stairs slowly, carefully, while keeping his mouth affixed to mine. Making our way through my bedroom door, he sets my legs back to the floor, and I push off of his mouth, standing directly in front of him.

I keep his gaze locked in before grabbing my shirt by the hems and stretching it over my head. I stand there in my sheer, laced bra and jeans. He takes a step towards me, gripping the back of my neck, kissing me gently as he moves his other hand to my breast. He slowly grazes his thumb over the thin lace covering my nipple as his tongue rolls with mine. Both hands move to the back of my bra, unhooking the clasp with a little work before he takes a step back to look. This being the first time he's seen me exposed like this.

"Fuck," he mutters as his hand grips his jaw.

His eyes sketch every inch of my body before he hastily presses his lips back onto mine, only for a moment before he kisses my chin, then dives into my neck. His tongue traces my skin with every kiss, and I whimper as his teeth slightly graze the flesh on my neck. He moves to my chest, lower and lower, until he sweeps my nipple into his mouth, his tongue circling and flicking me as I throw my head back and moan. He moves to the other breast, paying as much attention to it as he did the other. I move my hands to his cheeks, only to pull him up back to my lips. I want to taste him. I can't get enough. He unbuttons my jeans and hooks his thumbs into the sides, pulling them down over my hips. He releases from my lips, only to rest his forehead on mine and glance down at my panties to see them before pulling those down slowly. He lifts his eyes to mine through his lashes and kneels down to bring my thong to my ankles. He grips my ass and dips his head between my legs, giving me only a short moment to part for him before his mouth falls on my pussy. His tongue spreads me, and I groan as I feel him glide up to my clit. I spread my legs further for him as my head falls back, and my hands grip the back of his head to push him further into me.

"You taste so fucking good," he moans as his tongue moves up and down, tracing my slit.

He circles around my clit, licking in rhythm, and I grind my hips to push him harder into me. The wetness slapping against his tongue fills my ears and sends me into ecstasy. A loud moan escapes me as I thrust my hips more, speeding up the pace on his tongue.

"I'm coming," I groan with my teeth clenched.

He moans, and the sound of it alone pushes me over the edge. My body shakes as I tighten, slowing the rhythm of my hips down as I finish.

My body weak as he stands up, meeting my mouth with his again, this time so I can taste myself. He picks me up, throwing my legs around his waist as he turns and swings me onto my bed, laying me down. He lifts his shirt over his head, now only in his jeans and a brown belt. He leans down and dips his tongue back inside my mouth as his fingers meet my inner thigh. He slowly traces my skin until he reaches my clit, gently circling it as his lips dance with mine, his tongue rolling against me at every kiss. His finger pushes inside of me, causing me to groan into his mouth. I push off his lips to glance down at his finger thrusting inside of me. Our eyes lock as my mouth hangs open. He imitates me involuntarily and unclenches his jaw, letting it fall open, too, as I moan each time he pushes deep in. He speeds up, pushing further in as I whimper. He gently pulls out, only to fit two fingers inside of me. I look at him, his eyes locked on mine as he smiles, and I can see my wetness on the stubble surrounding his mouth. I smile back at him before moaning once he pushes both fingers in, over and over again. I can hear how wet I am and can feel with every push inside it splashes onto me. I've never felt this before. I've never been *this* wet.

"Vivian," Matt breathes heavily. "If you keep coming, I'm not going to last long," he smiles slightly. "But I promise I'll fuck you again, okay?" he says before crashing his lips on mine again, only for a moment. He rests his forehead hard against my own to sturdy himself, pushing harder into me, and I grab the back of his soft, teased hair and tug.

"I'm coming," I cry out.

He keeps his rhythm with his fingers inside of me. Moaning with me. My hips slow down as I try to catch my breath. My heart pounding out of my chest. He stands up straighter, pulling his jeans down with his white boxers. His thick cock, fully erect. I stare at it, hungry for him inside of me. He moves over my body, spreading my legs so his arms can hold them. On his knees, he moves his body closer to me. He places his cock on top of me, rubbing my clit with it, spreading my wetness on him so he can fill me with ease. I push up on my elbows to watch and moan at the tantalizing feeling.

"Fuck," he groans, rubbing against me, going faster, only edging his cock along my slit. His eyes roll while his head tilts back. "Fuck." He draws out a longer groan.

His head moves forward back to me, and his eyes scream desperation. His body twitches as his hot come spills out of him, coating my clit and pussy. He groans as his body shakes when he finishes, and he wipes the come off of the tip of his dick and slowly pushes into me. I don't have a second to think before he thrusts into me, and I cry out. He leans towards me, dropping his hands by my head as he pounds into me. He fills my mouth with his tongue and plunges into me faster, moaning into me as my nails grip his back.

I move my mouth from his, nudging him to flip over. He grabs my waist and swings us so I'm straddling him. I move my hips as I feel him throbbing inside of me. I grab my breasts and squeeze them with my hands as I watch him look at me. His eyes filled with desire, and he grips my hips to lift me slightly, only so he can thrust into me harder. I fall on top of him, my hair in his face and my hands around his head. My stomach raised from his as he pounds into me over and over again. I feel my core tighten, and the heat begin.

"I'm coming," I moan into his neck, almost crying out.

"Come, baby," he breathes back as I whimper, releasing my orgasm fully. He grunts as he lifts me off of his hips, bringing his hand to his cock to stroke himself as he comes again.

We stay for a moment — not moving, only breathing, before I roll to the free side of my bed, laying flat on my back. Both of us unable to catch our breath until I let out a small laugh.

"Holy shit," I say, the sweat beads on my skin.

He lets out a deep laugh followed by a sigh, turning his naked body towards mine. He wraps his arm around me and pulls me closer to him. I turn over so he spoons me, and we lay in silence as our breaths slow down. My stomach still fluttering, and my heart still pounding heavily. I grab his hand around my chest and observe it, lightly tracing my fingers on him. Observing every vein, every line on his fingernails and palm. I kiss his hand and tuck it back into me as I nestle my body against his and close my eyes, slowly drifting to sleep in what feels like complete euphoria.

A euphoria that seemed to only last a second before I hear Matt's voice over the jarring noise of my alarm.

"Vivian," he says again as he nudges my arm.

I dart my eyes open, smacking my hand on my nightstand to grab my phone and hit snooze. I shift my body to lay flat on my back as I turn my head to look at him.

"Good morning," he says with a smile, both of us still fully nude.

"I have to be at work in an hour," I groan with a wave of disappointment washing over my face.

"I'll get the shower started." Matt grins, and I smile back, ready for whatever he wants to give me.

CHAPTER TWENTY-ONE

I *can't focus. I can't focus at all today.*

"Welcome to Birch Books," I say to the customer who just walked in. I'm physically at work — mentally, my mind is shifted to the past fifteen hours with Matt.

"When is Alana Debose going to be here for the book signing?" She asks me.

"Hmm?" I say, trying to focus my mind back on her. "I'm sorry, I didn't hear you."

"When was Alana going to be here?"

"Oh, so sorry. Two weeks, on Thursday," I say with a smile.

"Thank you." She places her books on the counter for me to ring up. All I hear is the sound of beeping as my mind drifts again.

Beep.

Wet.

Beep.

Tongue.

Beep.

Moaning.

Beep.

"That'll be thirty-four dollars, and twenty-two cents, please," I snap out of my daze. I've got to shift my mind to something else. I can't just sit here all day thinking about Matt and our shower, or even last night, for that matter.

Matthew: I got called in tonight. I'm off next Tuesday. Dinner at my place?

Shit. That's four days from now. I can't go four whole days like this. I can't even fucking think straight. I text him back ***absolutely,*** then pull up my messages with Lauren.

Me: Sleepover tonight?
Lauren: Yay! Text me when you leave work

Good, this should help take my mind off of things. Besides, I have to fill her in on all the details. Well, maybe *not all.*

"Vivy." I hear Bill call from the back. I turn my head around to see if he says anything else. After a brief moment, I head through the curtain and into his office.

"How can I forward this email?" he asks with his glasses on the tip of his nose, stretching his neck to view the computer screen closer. I laugh quietly to myself and walk behind his desk. Leaning in to show him where to click. He taps my hand lightly, thanking me for my service. He thinks I'm some sort of wizard when I show him things like this.

"Vivy, sit," he says, extending his hand to point at the chair across from him. "I just wanted to tell you before you leave today how much Caroline and I appreciate you being here." *I smile.* "Ever since the day you walked into our lives, every day has been a blessing. Well, I guess I, I just wanted to say we love ya, Vivy. And you're doing a great job here. We're amazed at all you've accomplished in your life, especially without much guidance. I know your parents would be so proud of you. We sure are."

My eyes are heavy with tears forming. I blink, and they fall gently.

"Oh, Bill," I say as my lip quivers. I rush behind his desk and give him a hug. He has no idea how much that means to me. My mom was the last person to say she was proud of me. That was when I was eleven and made the volleyball team. *Everyone who tried out made the volleyball team.*

I let go of his hug, wiping the tears with my long sleeves.

"I didn't mean to make you cry, Vivy. I'm sorry," Bill says with sincerity in his voice.

"They're happy tears, Bill." I try to put a smile on.

Caroline comes in with a box of tissues. "We mean every word, Vivian."

I grab a couple from the box she's holding and blow my nose. Discarding it in the trash next to Bill's desk.

"I love you guys."

"We love you too, Vivy," they both reply.

"Okay. I've got to clean up before I leave." I wave my hands in front of my face to dry my eyes. I give Caroline a hug on my way out and head back to the front. Locking the door and switching the sign. I pick up the books that are lying around and organize others. Sending Lauren a quick text in between.

Me: Leaving in 10

I continue picking up and wiping down, sniffling my nose now and then to help dry my tears, and then I print off the figures for today before bringing them in back to Bill's office.

"Nice day today," I say as I lay them down next to him. "I'll see you guys both tomorrow!"

"Bye, darling," Caroline says.

"Goodbye, dear," Bill replies.

I make my way out of the front door and start my walk home. Stopping by a local mart to grab some wine for us. I arrive at my house and get in, placing the wine on the kitchen island and grabbing some blankets out of the cabinet near my stairs. I hear a knock at my door, followed by Lauren letting herself in.

"Hello," she sings.

"Look what I got." I sing back to her, dancing with the bottle of wine in my hand.

"I'm going to change." I hand her the wine and turn to walk upstairs.

She nods and walks to the kitchen. "I'll get us glasses."

I quickly grab a light blue cami and matching sleep shorts and head back downstairs. Lauren is curled on the couch with my TV already on, and my gray faux fur blanket draped over her, wine glass in her hand.

"I'm so excite,." I squeak giddily while climbing under the blanket next to her, grabbing the wine she poured me from the coffee table.

"Me too!" She expresses. "Can we try Gino's tonight? I've been dying for some lasagna?"

"Oh my god, you read my mind." I laugh, and I bring my phone up from the couch to place our order.

"So, tell me everything," she says, shifting her body to face me directly. "How did the date go?"

"It went...*well*." I grin so wide she knows it went more than well.

"Spill it," she presses.

I smile a bit wider, teeth showing in all their glory.

"Vivian," she shrieks, and I laugh, knowing she's impatient.

"It went *so* well," I say, raising my eyebrows.

"How was it...I mean, how was *he*?"

"*So. Fucking. Good,*" I enunciate to her slowly. I take a sip of my wine as her mouth drops slightly. "I've never come that much in my life, just in one night." I take another sip, and her mouth falls even further. "And then in the shower..." I drift off. Her mouth fully dropped, with the corners of her lips turned up in a smile. "Lauren, I'm not being funny here...I'm going to marry that man one day."

She laughs lightly, her smile beaming. "I'm so fucking happy for you."

I continue to gloat about our night..and morning, of course, as we find a movie to put on. Gino's arrives, and after finishing our dinner, we realize our entire bottle of Chardonnay has been drunk.

"I'll order another," Lauren announces as she takes the last bit of a sip from her glass. My phone dings in my hands.

Matthew: I cannot stop thinking about you.

My heart flutters, and my eyes soften. A smile spreads to my cheeks.

"Matt?" Lauren asks with a grin. I nod.

We spend the rest of our evening polishing off the second bottle of wine we had delivered and falling asleep on the couch.

I awaken to her alarm blaring on her phone, opening my eyes to see the light pouring in from my windows. My eyes squinting and my head pounding. *Hangovers*. The fucking worst.

I had promised her this morning I would go with her to help pick out invitation designs since I'm the maid of honor. She never actually *asked* me, though. It was just naturally assumed since she has no other close female friends in her life. Today will be difficult, I can already imagine. Lauren cares deeply about aesthetics, I, on the other hand, do not. She loves to mix and match colors I wouldn't even begin to think could go together. She has a natural eye for things like this, making it difficult for us to decide on something together. I can already hear her now... "Sangria or Burgundy?" when we both know it's just *maroon*.

CHAPTER TWENTY-TWO

T he rest of my weekend was filled with more wedding prep for Lauren. After choosing invitation colors, *she chose mahogany* — the next day, she wanted my input on venues. I happily obliged, doting around town with her, Carter, and Carter's best man Andrew. She didn't care much for any venues we saw, but I couldn't help her on Monday since I had to work. But now, it's Tuesday, *Matt's day off*. He told me to come over as soon as I'm finished with work, and to say I'm counting down by the second, is just putting it lightly. I try to breeze through the day, helping Bill and Caroline in the back, and helping customers out front. Going through the motions until I can see Matt again, more specifically, *Matt naked again*. I did get a photo of him at work, though. Friday night, after I was a bottle of wine deep, I snapped him a pic of me with my shirt up in the bathroom mirror, no bra on. He returned the favor by sending me a selfie, him in his scrubs with his shirt pulled up partially and his scrub pants pulled down a little lower than normal, giving me just enough of a view to see his toned stomach and an even better view of the lines forming a *V* that shape right down to that perfect cock of his. I saved the photo for a rainy day.

My shift is almost over, and I could not be any more ready to leave.

"Dear, can we order more of Richard Thompson's books?" Caroline asks while making her way up front to me.

"I just ordered them about thirty minutes ago," I say with a smile. I knew she was going to ask at some point, and I'm not trying to further delay my time here today. So everything they could possibly need or want done is already taken care of. "Do you need me to do anything else before I leave?"

"No, no, dear, you have a good night." I smile and grab my leather jacket and walk toward the door. "Say hello to Matty for me."

I turn to look at her, her face with a sly grin. I smile as my cheeks begin to warm like she caught me red-handed.

"See you tomorrow, Caroline." I blow her a kiss and walk out of the door, making sure it shuts tightly behind me. I walk towards Matt's house, noticing the leaves on the trees changing color even more. I come up to his apartment building and try to remember where I'm going. *Down the hall and to the left, fourteenth floor.* The familiar glass art cases the walls as I work my way up to him. 1415, I knock on the door.

"Come in. It's open!" Matt calls from inside. I push the door open, walking into the living area. I hear light music playing, and I see Matt taking ingredients out of the refrigerator and placing them on his center island. I smile, my eyes somewhat confused. "I figured we could learn how to cook tonight," he says, extending his hand to show off everything he got.

"You know, for our future kid's sake." He laughs. I grin wide, making my way next to him. "We're going to make honey garlic chicken and rice. The recipe says it's easy, so I thought that would be a good start for us," he says as he scrolls through the website on and iPad.

"Okay, let's do this." I clasp my hands together.

We read through together, my arms rested on the side of the island, he hunched over a bit as we share the screen. Preheat the oven, got it. Whisk the sauce in a bowl. How do you whisk? We take a moment to find the tool to whisk, then continue. I cut the chicken as he heats the pan with oil, we throw the chicken in, he flips that while I start on the rice. At least the rice is microwaved. I help Matt with a few more steps, and viola, *complete*. "That's it?" I laugh.

"That's it," he says after he tops my plate of rice off with the chicken.

We walk towards his dining table in the corner. The sky grows darker as the city lights of Boston grow brighter. I set my plate down and have a seat. He sets his plate down to get us something to drink.

"Wine?" he asks.

"Water is fine," I reply. He brings our glasses back, and we clink them, toasting each other before taking a sip. We dive in, eating and congratulating ourselves on our hard work. Well..it wasn't *that* hard, but I had fun, and it was nice to cook, especially with him. We talk about work as the sky becomes shaded even more, making each building stand out. I look around, observing the glass walls, looking at the city, and staring at Matt. My mental camera would be taking a thousand photos if I had one right now. Our conversation continues as we eat. I watch him, and his lips look soft, the way he opens his mouth before he takes a bite is slow, almost sensual-like, without meaning to be. When he laughs, his grin grows wide, his white teeth shining. The way he closes his mouth after he smiles makes his lips purse, the small lines that form enunciate the hardly visible scar by his top lip.

We finish up eating, both moving to the kitchen to put our plates in the sink.

"Want me to wash these?" I ask as I point to them, turning the faucet on.

"No, you don't need to," he says, hugging me from behind after he shuts the water off.

He wraps his arms around my waist, surrounding my body with his. He kisses the side of my head before sweeping my hair around my ear, exposing my neck for him. He kisses the dip between my neck and shoulder, slightly grazing his tongue on my skin. I sigh, tilting my head further to expose my neck more. He kisses me again with more heat, breathing heavily through his nose as he does. I moan quietly as his teeth gently drag on me.

He moves his hands to my breasts, holding them outside of my brown ribbed dress as he massages them gently. His mouth presses on my neck as his tongue becomes more prominent, and I tilt my head back in bliss, landing in the crook near his collarbone. He pulls the square neck of my dress down, exposing my breasts fully, and I tilt my chin back down to look. He squeezes lightly — circling and toying with my nipples, and I sigh a thick breath that was lodged in my throat. He turns me around to face him, pushing my back to the sink as he lifts me, so my legs wrap around his waist. He spins to face the island, taking steps towards it to set me down on top of the cold countertop. My legs still wrap around him as he takes my nipple into his mouth. His warm tongue caresses me as his lips tug gently at my pale pink bud — teasing me every so often when he lightly brushes only his lips against me.

"Take this off," he demands in a heavy breath, reaching the hem of my dress, and helping me pull it over my head.

He kisses my stomach, then plants another kiss near my hip, slowly hooking his fingers into the straps of my thong so he can pull them off. I wiggle — tilting my body from side to side, helping him get them off of me. As soon as he slides the remaining strap from my leg, he looks to the right, grabbing the bottle of honey next to me. He opens it, and he locks in my gaze, his eyes flamed with heat as he pours the honey on the top of my collar bone. It drips down, creating a steady stream over my breasts before he squirts some more near my belly button, letting it run down between my legs. It feels thick and cold as it moves slowly down my body. I spread my legs open further, leaning back slightly on the counter to give him better access. He leans into me before opening his mouth and dragging his tongue on my skin. Licking the honey around my nipples, he takes precious time to make sure every bit is completely sucked off. He moves slowly, with purpose, down to my belly. Working down even further while he closes his mouth each time in a kiss. He licks again, this time at the honey from the inner corner of my hips. He spreads my legs even more before grabbing onto the backs of my thighs to tilt my lower half up. He moves his mouth closer while he licks the honey dripping in the crevice between my thigh and pussy. I whimper at the feeling of his tongue barely hitting my clit. He does it again before he moves over, placing his mouth on me fully. Sucking and teasing my clit. His mouth filling with me and honey at the same time. He flicks my clit with his tongue as he inserts two fingers deep inside of me. I throw my head back as I moan loudly, not able to keep quiet. He thrusts his fingers as I rock my hips with him, letting him get deeper. I feel myself filling up, ready to explode. I shut my eyes as I move my hips faster, riding his face and fingers.

"I'm coming!" I cry out.

He moans as my body contracts against him. He lifts his head up to have his mouth meet mine again, kissing me with nothing less than pure passion. He escapes from my lips only for a moment to undress. Throwing his shirt to the ground and hastily unbuttoning his pants before pushing them down after. I take in the sight of him, fully erect already, and it sends more heat to my core.

He possesses my mouth again before he lifts me up, my legs draped over the bend in his arms as his thick cock slides into me with ease. He backs away from the counter, holding me as if I'm as light as a feather. His hands grip my lower back as he thrusts into me, pounding me over and over — faster and harder each time. He groans as he dives his hot tongue into my mouth, grazing it against mine. Our lips hardly connecting from the relentless thrusting.

"Fuck!" I cry out as he continues to fill me.

He walks us to the couch slowly. As he pounds steadily into me, the sound of my wet pussy slapping against him fills the room. He lays me down over the arm rest and slips out of me, placing his mouth back on my throbbing clit. I grab the top of his hair, gripping each strand in-between my fingers, keeping him there long enough for me to come again. I grab his face and pull him upwards, giving me enough room to stand in front of him. The entire city of Boston shines in the darkness behind him as I kneel in front of him. I wrap my hands as much as I can around his cock before I open my mouth slightly to run my tongue along his length. He groans as my tongue reaches his tip, and his eyes stay locked on mine. I wrap my lips around him, taking him as far back as I can go as my eyes flutter shut. He grunts loudly as he places one hand behind my head, gripping the back of my hair as he pushes my head into him softly while he thrusts into my mouth.

"Oh my god," he moans as I continue to suck him.

I look up at him, his eyes still directly on me. I keep our gaze intact as I open my mouth wide, exposing his sight to see my tongue flat — pressing against him. He grins, almost mischievously, then rolls his eyes in ecstasy as he sighs.

I spit on his cock with the saliva built up and stroke it with my hand, bringing my other hand up to help. He grunts again as I move both hands against him, flicking my wrist and holding firmly. My breasts, moving with my body, sit in between my arms, and I know his view of them pressed together from above is making him throb. I can feel him in my hands, growing harder if at all possible.

"Keep going, baby," he pleads as I continue stroking him, speeding up slightly.

I moan and look at how he fills my hands, so much so, my fingers can't wrap around him.

"I'm gonna come," he groans.

I continue only for a short moment before his hot come drips out, running down my knuckles onto my wrists. It's warmer than the honey and moves faster too. I look up at him and smile as he tries to catch his breath, panting vigorously. I let go of him, slowly coming to a stand. He grabs my waist and brings me in to kiss me, my hands draped with his semen still.

"Let's clean up," I breathe into his mouth before kissing him with a peck.

He squeezes my ass before walking with me to his bathroom and starting the shower. I climb in once it's warm enough, and he follows, grabbing the soap and a loofah before he suds it up and places it on my chest. He rubs the loofah over my breasts, rubbing in circular motions, coating my skin with bubbles. He moves down to my stomach, sweeping it between my legs gently, and I sigh at the sensation of the coarse mesh as it grazes me. He brings his lips to mine, gently parting my mouth with his tongue. I take the loofah and run it along his body like he did for mine. We rinse off together as my arms drape across his neck, and our eyes remain stuck on each other. He cups my face in his hands and gently brushes his nose against mine. The heat of his breath mixes with my own, and the steam from the shower moves all around us.

"I think I'm falling in love with you, Vivian," he whispers to me.

My gleaming eyes tilt up to his. I smile as I lean in for a kiss, and our lips touch softly. Every time he kisses me, my heart flutters as if it's dropping. His lips are smooth and full, and the use of his tongue is never overdone, never assaulting. Everything about him is something I've dreamed of, my entire life, that only seemed to happen in movies and books or to everyone else... *but me*.

"I think I'm falling in love with you too, Matt," I reply.

We embrace each other for a while as the hot beads of water cascade down our skin. We finally get out and grab towels before he throws me a Boston University T-shirt from his closet, along with a pair of white boxer briefs. I dry off and put them on, following his movements of throwing the extra pillows on his bed to the floor. He reaches for his corner of the folded duvet, and I reach for mine, both of us tossing it loose before sliding into bed. He grabs me and yanks me close to him, tucking my body against his so he overpowers me, spooning me tightly.

"Please stay all day tomorrow," he groans softly into my ear. "I have to go to work just for a bit, but I want you to stay and sleep here again."

I smile, my head still turned away from his.

"*Please,*" he begs again.

I grin and agree before my eyes fall heavy, and my mind drifts to sleep right in his arms.

CHAPTER TWENTY-THREE

"Coffee is done, I'll be back around two o'clock. Miss you already," is what the note on the kitchen island says. I hold it for a moment as my elbows rest on the counter, staring at his messy handwriting. Why is every doctor's handwriting *messy*? The light shines through the windows so intensely you would think it was a summer day. I look around, realizing how weird it is in his place, alone. Of course, I'm going to snoop around. I just need coffee first.

I open the cabinet to grab a mug before I pour the coffee in. Sipping as I lean on the counter, looking around at his apartment. I'm not really sure where I should look first or why I would be looking around. It seems only customary, though, to at least check out the medicine cabinet.

I push off the counter and walk to his bathroom, still sipping my black coffee as I open the bottom cabinet under the sink. *Toilet paper, mouthwash, cleaning supplies, first aid kit.*

Boring.

Moving on to the tall cabinet. *Toothbrush, toothpaste, cologne, deodorant, lotion, medicine, sunscreen.* I stand there, staring at the items. Nothing unusual or alarming, and *thank god* there are no traces of a woman ever being here.

I close the door and turn around. Shutting the bathroom light off, I move to his room. Working my way to the closet to at least change my shirt. I rifle through the hangers, touching each shirt lightly as I skim them. I run my fingers over the folded t-shirts, pulling out a navy one after I set my coffee down. I unfold it to see it's a Boston red socks shirt. I lift the shirt I have on over my head before throwing that on the floor, putting the new clean one on. I pick up the shirt from the ground and put it in the clothes hamper I saw in the bathroom. The red socks shirt is two sizes too big, but I can imagine on him. He fills it out completely. I grab my coffee and head back to the kitchen, grabbing my phone to call Lauren and tell her about last night.

"He said he loved you?" she asks excitedly.

"Well, not really...he said he *thought* he was falling in love with me."

"Viv, that's the fucking same thing. Did you say it back?"

"Yeah, I mean, I agreed..." I say before she interrupts.

"And now you're just...in his house, all day, *alone*?

"Yes." I giggle.

"Where have you looked first?"

"Huh?" I ask. Knowing damn well what she said.

"I know you're snooping..where did you look first?"

"Bathroom," I say flatly with a grin she can't see.

"Anything? Check his night stand." She laughs.

"Nothing. Okay, hold on, I'm going to keep you on the phone," I say as I walk back to his bedroom, bringing myself to his bedside table. I open the drawer and look. "Okay, a couple of books, phone charger, condoms."

"Condoms?" she snaps quickly. "How many?"

"I don't know. It's just a box. It's not opened."

"You didn't use a condom? Viv!"

"Yeah, yeah, preach to me later. I'm busy now," I say, continuing to look through. I grab the book on top and flip through, coming to the bookmarked page. "Oh my god, Lauren."

"What!" She shrieks.

"My note," I say quietly, staring at the napkin.

"You're what?" She replies loudly.

"My note from the hospital. It's his bookmark." I stare at the page with the folded napkin, the words *Thanks, Doc* written by me.

"He kept it?" she says with what seems to be a smile in her voice.

I shut the book, suddenly feeling terrible for looking around and invading his personal space. My heart flutters as I close the drawer before returning to the kitchen.

"I'm going to order some breakfast, Lo. I'll call you later," I say to her before hanging up. I stand in his kitchen, where he licked honey off me. Flashbacks flood my mind as I sip my coffee. I walk towards the living room, grabbing the remote before plopping myself on his light gray leather sectional. Turning on the TV, the news is at full volume, blasting loudly. I startle and laugh to myself, turning it down to a more respectable volume. My phone dings as I go to change the channel.

Matthew: Good morning. I hope you slept well. Don't leave. I'll be home later.

I don't know what he expects me to do all day. I mean...I had nothing to do anyway. I would have just sat at *my* house instead. I flip through my phone after I text him back and find some breakfast to order myself. I don't know his door code, so if I were to leave to grab something from the market down below, I wouldn't be able to get back in. So it looks like delivery all day for me. I place my order and find a movie to watch.

After I finish my coffee, I grab the throw blanket behind me and snuggle up, waiting for my food. What seems to be an hour goes by before the doorbell rings.

I spend most of the afternoon watching TV, scrolling through my phone, snacking on my breakfast leftovers, and relaxing. I can't hear the city sounds like I do at my place, but I take every chance I get to stand up and walk closer to the floor-to-ceiling windows covering the apartment's corner. Just standing there, taking in the city that I've grown to love so much. I often miss Chicago, but the thought of returning is just too detrimental for me. I'm not sure I'll ever visit again. No one is there waiting for me anyways.

As I'm looking out the window with my arms crossed in front of me, my phone chimes from the couch.

Matthew: I have to work a bit longer, but I promise I'm hurrying. I'll see you soon.

Well, shit. It's already one-thirty. I've spent the day being the most lazy version of myself, which I don't like to do. I just need to treat this as a vacation. Yeah, a vacation is all this is. I resume my positions, cuddling on the couch with his blanket tucked under me, wrapping me in my little cocoon. After two hours of Netflix and four episodes into a new crime series, I hear a faint knocking sound. I ignore it, assuming it was a noise from a neighbor. The knock comes again, louder, and I realize it's coming from Matt's door. I throw the blanket off of me and quickly walk to the door, swinging it open only to see a lengthy man in a gray beanie and glasses staring at me.

"Hello?" I say, a little confused.

"Hi," he replies, *actually* confused. "Is...Matt home?"

"No, sorry, not yet." I stand in the doorframe, my hair disheveled from last night and Matt's two sizes too big shirt on with nothing else.

"I came to pick up my toolbox I lent him. My name is Luke. Are you Vivian?" he asks with a slight smile. *How the hell does he know my name?*

"Yes?" I reply with confusion still written on my face.

"Can I...come in and grab that really quick?" he asks with a laugh after we had spent a full solid minute just staring at each other in silence.

"Oh yes, of course!" I snap out of it, grinning awkwardly as I open up the door further for him to walk in. He shuffles past me making his way through the corridor and into the open living area.

"I thought he would be home by now. Do you know where he might have put it?" he questions, working his way through the kitchen, putting his hands on the island counter right where my bare ass sat last night as Matt was working his tongue down my body. *Damn, these flashbacks.*

"No, sorry," I say to him. *Unfortunately, a tool box was not something I found while I was snooping through his personal belongings.*

"That's all right. It's gotta be somewhere around here." Luke places his hands on his hips, staring intensely around the apartment. I grab my water bottle from the counter and take a sip. "So, are you guys living together now?" He opens the cabinets below the island countertop.

"Are we what?" I spit my mouthful of water onto the floor.

"Living together, you know...since you're here." He chuckles, still looking inside the bottom cabinets.

"No..." I trail off.

"Oh, I'm sorry, it's just — Matty doesn't bring girls here, and the man hasn't had a girlfriend in the past five years I've known him. The way he talks about you two, I just —

assumed." He staggers as he closes the cabinets, opening the ones next to it.

"He doesn't bring girls here?" I ask, stunned.

"No." He laughs. "Never."

"Does he really talk about me *that* much?" I ask.

"Oh yeah." He smiles. "Shit, ever since you hit him with your car, it's been nonstop, Vivian this, Vivian that. Hell, on my *birthday,* he ditched me to hang out with you. And he's my best friend." He grins, then finds the toolbox before standing up straight to look at me. "He really likes you, Vivian," he says with a pressed smile, his grey eyes piercing mine. "Don't hurt the guy, please." His eyes soften. He swallows hard and continues, "He's been through a lot. I know you have to, or...so I hear. Just, he's got to be in love with you. He's never talked about a girl the way he's talked about you. You should see his face light up when he does. I mean, hell, I knew what your eyes looked like before I ever saw them in person."

I stand there, completely astonished. Happiness caresses my skin with a warm sensation. He doesn't bring girls here, hasn't had a girlfriend in *how* long, and he's begging *me* not to leave?

"What did he say when he first met me?" I smile, walking to the barstool and taking a seat, trying to get every bit of information I can out of Luke.

"Since your car flung into his?" He laughs, setting the toolbox down in front of me on the counter. "Well, let's just say he hasn't shut up since. You seem really great, Vivian, and I can promise you, you've made him much happier since the day he met you." He gazes down at his hands. "But I better shut up before I keep spilling his secrets." He laughs. "Sorry to barge in here. Thanks again." He holds up the toolbox and makes for the door.

"It was nice meeting you, Luke!" I say as he walks away.

He stops and turns to me and says, "It was really nice meeting you, Vivian."

As I hear the front door shut, my stomach is whirling, and my heart is racing. *He talks about me..a lot.* I smile, sitting at the island. My stomach swirls again, this time with hunger. I glance at the clock on the stove. Four, *shit*, I need to eat. I grab my phone, and instead of ordering delivery, I order groceries. Items needed for a recipe I just found for cajun chicken pasta. The least I could do is be useful and make dinner for us. I enlarge the recipe on his iPad and look around for the pots and pans I need while I wait for the groceries to come. I get to work as soon as they arrive, following exact measurements and instructions. My phone dings right as I'm stirring the pasta. I reach over and grab it to see Matt had texted.

Matthew: Leaving in 20, be there soon.

I finish combining the ingredients and stare at my masterpiece. I grab a fork to take a bite right from the pan. It's good. I mean, *really* good. I smile, impressed with myself. I plate our dinners and put them on the dining table. Cleaning up the debris and seasonings sprawled out. I put a lid on the pan with the remaining pasta and fill two glasses with water as I hear the front door unlock.

"Viv?" he calls from the corridor.

"In here!" I say as I set the water down on the counter.

He comes into the kitchen, smiling brightly. He's wearing dark blue scrubs and looking as handsome as ever. He walks towards me, sweeping his hand to the back of my neck, kissing me softly as he pulls my body closer to his. His tongue flirting with the skin on my lips.

"You made dinner?" He grins while pulling his lips back.

I shake my head yes and kiss him again, wrapping my arms around him and threading my fingers through his hair.

"Thank you for staying." He sighs against my mouth as his lips move with mine. His body is so close that I can feel him getting harder under his scrub pants. He pushes his body gently on mine so my back hits the counter. His tongue enters my mouth as I part my lips for him. He tastes sweet, and his tongue is hot against mine. He moans lightly before parting his mouth from me.

"What are you doing to me, Vivian?" he whispers with his forehead pressed against mine, lightly grazing his nose with me.

I can feel him fully erect against me. I move my hips slightly to cause friction between us. He closes his eyes for a moment and breathes, before taking my mouth against his, pulling my thong off, and tugging his pants down just above his knees. He lets go of my mouth only to take his shirt off, and as soon as they're around his ankles, he parts my legs by lifting one up to the side and slowly guiding his cock to my entrance. He tries to push in slowly to no avail before backing up slightly to look me in my eyes and spit into his hand, rubbing it against his cock before he thrusts into me. I moan, my lips falling open again. He lifts my shirt up and brings his mouth to my nipple, sucking and pulling at it as his tongue flicks it. His hips move slowly, making sure I take every inch of him. The deeper he goes, the more I cry out. I can already hear how wet I am, as does he. He groans as he looks down, making sure he can see just how far he is inside of me. He looks at me. His blazing brown eyes pierce mine, and his jaw drops slightly. We hold our gaze as he plunges into me, and I whimper at every move—our breathing audibly loud.

I can feel my pulse through my chest as I lock onto the back of his hair, tugging gently at it. We rest our foreheads together, our lips barely touching, only lightly grazing with each thrust. The sound of him groaning alone sends me over the edge into another orgasm, and I grip his shoulders as my head falls back. He speeds up his rhythm inside of me as I come. His groans get louder and louder as he pulls out of me quickly, in hardly enough time before his come drips on the floor. His firm grasp on my thigh he was holding up only becomes tighter as he finishes. He drops my leg once he's done, and we both try to slow our breathing. He looks at me with fire in his eyes, and kisses me so passionately I have no choice but to assume its love.

Everything about him drives me crazy.

And I know there's no turning back now.

CHAPTER TWENTY-FOUR

I thought meeting Alana Debose was going to be exciting, but now that she's here at Birch Books, it's actually quite the opposite. She's been nothing but demanding. Especially to Caroline, which, I'm sorry, I will not stand for. I don't fight, I'm usually not one for confrontation, but if Alana rolls her eyes one more time regarding Caroline's questions, I *will* shove her into the bookcase with my hand around her throat. *What a bitch.*

"I need water, not tap. Has to be a bottle," she demands.

I think the fuck not, Alana. I would rather shit on my hand.

"We don't have bottled water. But feel free to go to the gas station on the corner," I say with a sarcastic grin, turning from her and heading in back.

The past nine days have flown by. Between *pure heaven* with Matt, wedding planning with Lo, and getting ready for this horrid wench at Birch Books now, my days have quickly moved past.

"She's terrible, ain't she?" Caroline asks as soon as I enter the office.

"Horrible." I scoff, shutting the door. We all laugh, but truthfully, there's nothing funny about having to spend the next two hours with her here. I hear the bell ring above the door and dart back to the front. The book signing isn't until twenty more minutes, so I thought I had enough time to talk shit about Alana, with Bill and Caroline beforehand. I open the curtain and see Matt walking in. Alana no where to be found.

"Hi." I smile. He grins as we move closer together, his thumb and index finger grabbing my chin so I can meet his lips.

"Bill in the back?" he asks.

"Yep, waiting for you."

"Is that author here yet?"

"Don't even get me started." I roll my eyes.

He chuckles and kisses me with a peck before walking in the back. I make my way behind the counter as the bell rings above the door again. Only this time, it's Satan's spawn. She looks at me, smug-like, as she moves behind the table to sit and await her cult following.

The hours go by painfully slowly as she reads a portion of her new book, takes questions, snaps photos, and signs her books. I kept sneaking in back with Caroline to watch the boys play poker. But now, thankfully, she's finished.

"Have a good night." Alana grabs her bag and leaves. That was probably the nicest thing she's said to me all evening. I walk in back to let everyone know we're in the clear.

"She's gone," I sing with a grin. Caroline cheers as Matt and Bill laugh while holding their cards. "I'm going to head out. Does anyone need anything before I go?" I say, mainly speaking to Bill and Caroline.

"No, dear, you've done enough today. We will see you on Monday," Caroline states as Bill agrees.

"We're almost done, then I'll be over, okay, Viv?" Matt says as he places chips in the middle of the desk.

"Okay," I smile and wave goodbye. "See you guys on Monday."

I try to get home quickly because my room is a mess, and there's no way in hell Matt should ever see it like this. Between going back and forth from both of our places and finding dressy clothes for Lauren's events, my bedroom floor has seemed to collect all the scraps from things I never wore. The things I violently threw to the ground because they didn't fit right.

I open my front door and run in, picking up whatever is lying around. I fold my throw blanket and press it neatly to my couch. Heading into the kitchen, I put the dirty dishes in the dishwasher and shove a couple of bills in a drawer. I run upstairs to tackle my bedroom, completely forgetting I haven't even made my bed. Once I'm finished tidying up, I make my way downstairs to pop open a bottle of wine and grab a glass. My doorbell rings, and I call to Matt that it's unlocked. He comes in, holding another bottle of wine. I turn to face him, pouring already.

"Well, you have a backup now." He laughs as he sets the bottle he bought on the counter.

"Chinese or Thai tonight?" I ask.

"I was thinking dessert first?" He smirks, grabbing my chin and bringing my lips to his, planting a large kiss on me.

"Matt, I'm hungry," I groan in a laugh.

"Okay, okay, food first, desert right after." He agrees.

I nod, and I take a sip of my wine. We make our way to the couch, with tonight's plan being takeout, Netflix, and sex, *lots of sex*. I place the order on my phone as Matt looks for our movie feature of tonight, landing on a comedy. We snuggle up, I sip my wine, and we laugh as the movie goes.

Only pausing to get the food from the door and to steal kisses every now and again.

"What do you want to put on now?" he asks as the movie ends, our stomachs full of Thai.

"Rom-Com?" I suggest. He flips through, finding one we both agree on as I lay back down with my leg stretched across him. He rubs my foot gently like he's been doing for the past thirty minutes.

"I swear I could do this forever," he says with his eyes on the TV and a wide grin on his face.

"Me too, Matt." I smile, my lips pressed in a curl and one arm under my head with my sight directed firmly at him.

I sit up to get closer to him, pressing my body against his as I fold my hands on his shoulder, still looking at the side of his face. He turns his head and smiles, kissing me on the forehead.

"You're really the most beautiful person I've ever laid eyes on," he says softly. I smile as I lean in, kissing him gently while I grab the side of his face.

"My parents would have loved you." I gaze into his eyes, my hand pulling away from him. He rubs his thumb on my cheek, caressing me gently. His eyes are soft and comforting.

"How did it happen?" he says in a whisper, a whisper I almost didn't catch. He moves his hand away from my face and shifts his body a little toward me.

I slightly turn my head to the side, not fully understanding the question.

"How did they pass?" he asks a little louder. I look down, focusing on the blanket on top of us. Only for a moment to gain my composure.

"My dad died of natural causes, I guess you could say. He had a bad heart, and he was getting older. My mom..." I pause to breathe. *This isn't usually a conversation I enjoy having*. "My mom actually died here, in Boston." I look at him. "She was on a work trip, and..um, she got into a car accident. She was t-boned."

He reaches for my hand. Saying it out loud sends a sting to my chest. This might be the first time I realize my mother's car and mine were hit the same way, but only one of us is still here.

"I don't know." I wipe a tear falling on my cheek. "I've just been so angry about the whole thing, the way it happened. I mean, who the fuck gets drunk on a Tuesday night, crashes into a car, and doesn't stop to call anyone. Doesn't stop to help. I mean, for fucks sake, it wasn't even the fourth of July yet! Why couldn't they wait to party until then," I spout off, playing catch up with my fingers, wiping the tears away as they spill.

Matt lets go of my hand, bringing it to himself. Looking at me with vacant eyes and a stoic expression.

"How many years ago was this again?" His breath somewhat quiet as his eyebrows pinch together.

"I don't know, um, twelve." I wipe my nose with my napkin I'd used at dinner.

He takes a deep breath. Looking confused or lost, I can't tell the difference.

"Do you," he pauses, his breath shallow. "Do you know what color your mom's car was?" he asks, gulping dryly after the question.

"What?"

"What color was the car, Vivian," he demands firmly, clenching his jaw.

My pulse quickens. He hasn't snapped at me before. This hardly feels like the right time too.

"Red. It was red," I stammer.

He deepens his breath, as if needing air. His face grows white as if the blood has drained from him. Standing up quickly, he puts his hands on top of his head, pacing back and forth only a few steps.

"Fuck," he whispers, almost weeping.

"Matt?"

"Fuck," he weeps again.

"Matt!" I shout. Forcing him to stop and face me. His eyes squinted and red. His face pinched together, eyebrows burrowed. He brings his hands to the bridge of his nose and wipes it down as if gasping in between.

"Vivian, you have to listen to me." He shoots down to the couch, sitting next to me, grabbing my hand as if to plead. My heart is pounding. I stare at him, with nothing but confusion on my face. "Please, Vivian," he begs, his eyes welling with tears.

"What?" I breathe heavily.

Is this the bad, finally coming around to crash down on me? To show me that relationships like this only happen in the movies, that men like him don't actually exist, and that all of this is temporary.

"I think - I think my brother was the person who hit your mom."

"What?" I ask again, raising my eyebrow and sighing heavily.

"And I, I was in the car too." His eyebrows pinch as he stutters.

My heart drops suddenly. My pulse begging to push through my skin. My ears suddenly plugged with only a loud ring becoming present. I see Matt's lips move, but I can't hear anything. He's shaking my arms like he's pleading with me. I can't hear. I can't move. My body is numb, and that *fucking ringing* won't go away. I can't breathe. My chest won't allow the air to move. I stare, my eyes lifeless. The ringing fades, and I can slowly hear his voice again.

"Vivian, please, you have to understand," he begs.

"Get out," I finally muster.

He doesn't move. He doesn't answer.

"Get out!" I yell, standing up and pointing my finger to the door.

"Vivian."

"Get the fuck out!" I scream, my face red, my eyes pinched shut.

"I tried Vivian, I told you, I went back. Please!" He's begging, trying to grab my hands as I walk away towards the door.

"Leave Matt! Get the fuck out of my life!" I shout. The tears pour down my face. My heart is pounding—my chest piercing with pain while my stomach knots into oblivion.

I lost her. I lost so many years, memories, and moments when I needed *her*. I can't even comprehend what the fuck is happening.

His face, red and washed with tears like mine as he opens the door and walks out slowly, his posture hunched. Barely making it out of the door before I slam it shut. I wail as my back presses against it, and I slide down until I hit the floor.

I bring my knees to my chest and hug them as tightly as I can. Screaming in my own apartment. The ringing returning as my breaths get shorter. My whole heart shattered. I lay, still curled up with myself. Shutting my eyes as tight as they can go.

My whole future with him *gone*.

Every piece of my soul he had *gone*.

My love for him. *gone*.

CHAPTER TWENTY-FIVE

I don't think justice is ever served. No matter what the punishment is, it will never compare to how the victim or victim's family's lives will be forever changed because of one heinous act. My life forever altered because of two men. One I thought I might have fallen in love with.

I can't get out of bed. I've tried, sort of. The thought of eating isn't appealing, and I'd rather sleep than shower. My phone died because of all the text messages and calls that kept coming through *that I didn't answer.* I only used it once to call Caroline and take yesterday off. I wouldn't be of any use at the store anyways. My hands won't stop shaking. I try to close my eyes again as my doorbell rings. I don't move a muscle. I don't even flinch. It rings again, then again, until I hear it open. I shift my eyes slightly to my bedroom door. The only person who has a key besides me is Lauren. I hear her high heels hit my wood floors as she makes her way to the stairs.

"Vivian?" She gently opens my bedroom door.

I don't respond. I'm not in the mood to talk.

"Vivian, you need to get out of bed."

"No," I groan as I bury my face into my pillow. She takes the blankets off me, and I lay there...now cold.

"Let's get you something to eat." She sits on my bed, lifting my body up to put my arm around her. "Maybe a shower first." She grins slightly, trying to make me laugh. I take a deep breath and sit, hunched over. This is taking all of the energy I have right now.

"Why are you here?" I ask quietly.

"Well..you weren't answering your phone, and...Matt called me."

I shoot my eyes at her. Pulling slightly away.

"He told me what happened..." she continues. I look at her, still confused about what she could possibly say. "Viv, you really need to talk to him."

"What?" I snap. "About what? What could I possibly have to say to him?" My voice grows louder.

"Vivian, it was an accident. It wasn't his fault," she says, defending him like some lunatic.

"Are you kidding me?" I yell, standing up straight off the bed.

"He was fifteen, Viv..."

"So. Fucking. What." I scream.

"He tried to help.."

"No, he did *not*," I snap.

"Call him, Vivian, please."

The last fucking thing I want to do is hear his excuses. "I'm not. I seriously can not believe you are trying to defend him, Lauren." I throw my arms up, trying to figure out why she is taking his side.

"Vivian, listen to me!" she screams back at me, standing up and getting closer to my face. "He went to the police station! His brother was driving! He was just a kid!"

None of what she is saying makes me feel any better. In fact, it hurts even worse knowing she's trying to make it seem like this is something I should just blow over. How fucking insensitive, how fucking irrational.

I don't want to tell her to leave. I would never kick her out of my home. No matter how much I can't stand her right now, she's my best friend. I grab a sweatshirt from my closet and barge out of my room. Stomping my feet on the stairs as I descend. I put on my tennis shoes and slam the front door shut on my way out. Getting the hell away from anyone and everyone. I walk. Nowhere to go and not a plan in my head. I just walk. I put the hood of my sweatshirt up, keep my head down, and stick my hands in my pockets.

I walk for twenty, maybe thirty minutes. I'm not sure. My phone is dead, and I didn't bring it. I only glance up occasionally to check my surroundings. I keep going, walking past things I've already seen. Choosing left and right on a whim. I look up just to see my location. Birch Books falls in my line of sight. I look both ways and cross the street. Walking through the front door, my eyes land on Caroline first. Her face drops with a hint of sadness at the sight of me. I don't know what I look like, but it's enough for her to know I'm not okay. I keep my gaze on her as I swallow hard.

"Is Bill here?" I ask quietly. She nods gently, and I move towards the curtain, pushing through to walk to his office. I knock faintly before I open the door. My eyes meet Bill as he shifts slightly in his seat.

"Vivy?" he says with a shaky voice. "Is everything alright?"

My lip quivers as I walk in, taking a seat in the chair across from him. My eyes filling with tears.

"Can I talk to you about something?" I ask, almost in a whisper. Bill nods as his eyebrows pinch and his bottom lip pulls into his mouth.

I take a deep breath. "I found out that... Matt and his brother are responsible... for my mom's accident." My breath is shaking uncontrollably.

Bill's eyes drop to his hands that are folded on his desk. He takes a deep breath and asks, "How do you know?"

"He told me," I cry.

"Did he tell you what happened?" Bill asks gently in his raspy voice.

"I don't know," I say, the tears falling down my cheeks. "I didn't hear him. I just made him leave." My voice cracks as I sob, and I bring my hands to my face to catch the tears.

"Wow," he says, clearing his throat. "That's...that's tough, Vivian," he continues, not knowing how to handle the situation.

I continue to cry into my hands. The thought alone consumes my emotions. I had built up so much anger and resentment all these years. And to finally catch the guy, only to have it be one of the most heartbreaking truths I've ever heard.

"I don't...I don't know what to say, Vivy, but I can tell you that out of the seventy-nine years I've been alive, the one promise I made myself was to never carry hate in my heart. Carrying too much hate can weigh it down. But I know you, Vivy. Your heart is too good to harbor any hatred. Forgiveness is never easy. If it was, the world would be a much better place. Forgiving someone doesn't exonerate them for what they've done. Forgiving someone frees *your* soul that binds you to them. A clear heart and a free soul Vivy. That's what I live by."

I slowly stop crying… I listen, and hear him. My mind is racing with a million thoughts.

I lick my dry lips and stand up, walking behind the desk to give Bill a hug. The longest hug we've ever shared.

"Thank you," I whisper to him. "Love ya, Bill," I sniffle.

"Love you too, Vivy," he whispers while he pats my back gently. I walk out, moving through the front door. Caroline must have been in the bathroom, but I couldn't stay. I needed to leave right away. I walk down the street and notice the sun should be setting soon. I don't have my phone to order an Uber, so I try to flag down a taxi when I see one.

"Waterfront Park, please," I say to the taxi driver. Fishing out a twenty-dollar bill that I keep in my running shoes. I open the door after he parks and issue a thanks to him before I walk along the sidewalk and find a spot in the grass. I sit down and hug my knees to my chest and rest my head. My mind feels like it's unraveling — only it's knotted yarn, it can't unravel all the way, it can't process *anything*.

The feelings and emotions I have crash into each other like a tsunami. I let my tears fall as my sweatshirt catches them. I loved Matt. I *love* Matt. How can this be happening? Maybe I should have listened to him, but I couldn't process anything at the time. I threw him out of my house, the man I love, I threw him out. But I had every reason to, right? For years and years I have had so much hatred and anger settling inside of me for the person responsible. I think it's time to let it go. Sure, I might hear some more heartbreaking truths, but I would rather know the truth than live in a fairy tale lie.

I sit for a moment and listen to the faraway voices and the light sound of traffic coming from the street. I sit, under a tree, with hardly anyone near me.

I tilt my head to look at the water, only to see wisteria painting the sky.

Hi mom.

CHAPTER TWENTY-SIX

I 'm not sure how I got here. I blindly left the park, suddenly hopped in a cab, and landed in front of The Maison, *Matthew's apartment complex*. I walk in, nodding to the concierge before making my way to the elevators. Fourteenth floor. The door opens as I step out, walking down the hall. I stand in front of his door and take a breath. It's like my body brought me here without my brain having a say in what was happening. I knock on the door and wait...and wait.

No answer.

I knock once again, taking a small step back from the door. I stand, waiting still. He probably is working. I stand for a bit longer by his door until I decide to go home and charge my phone to reach him that way. I get back in the elevator and exit his building. I only had enough cash for those two cab rides, so I need to walk home. Luckily I'm used to this route and know my way back. I walk, watching the sky grow darker, and the street lights shine brighter. People all around, laughing, smiling, and enjoying each other's company in the city.

I don't even know why I went there, to his place. Maybe...maybe I need to hear what happened, not for his sake, but for my own. There were always questions and speculations about the other driver. Maybe it would benefit me know exactly how it happened, knowing every detail I can to piece it together. Maybe it'll make it worse. I don't know. But I need to hear it from Matt. I can't possibly fathom that the man he is today is the same man from twelve years ago. I wouldn't have fallen in love with him otherwise. I walk further, finally turning on my corner to where only the street lights guide me.

Coming up to my house, I see a figure sitting on my stoop, hunched over. I walk slower, trying to adjust my eyes to see who it is. The hood of the dark sweatshirt covers whoever face is hiding underneath. I walk up closer, and the sounds of my footsteps bring his eyes to mine.

"Matt?" I ask with a stuffy nose and a sniffle as he lifts his head up from his folded arms on his knees.

His face looks tired under the orange tint of the lights. The stubble on his face is more pronounced, as if he hasn't done anything with himself in days.

"Vivian, I just needed to talk to you." He stands up quickly from the steps, holding his arms out as if for me to stay put.

I take an involuntary step back at the quickness of him standing.

"Please don't go," he begs. His stature is different like his whole body is sorrowful. His eyes reek of misery. *I don't like seeing him this way.*

"I just came from your place, Matt," I mumble. "You weren't home...I came..to get my phone and call you," I continue softly, with as much heartache in my voice as he has. I walk closer to him and look up, staring right into his eyes.

He doesn't smile. There's no grin. His eyes look heavy, weighed down like an anchor at sea. I take a breath and swallow dryly.

"Come inside, please," I tell him, almost immediately regretting the words that came out of my mouth.

I don't know what I'm doing, and I'm second-guessing my idea to have any sort of conversation with him right now. We walk inside, and I sit on the couch, my hood still over my head as I grab a blanket and cover it over my legs, almost as a shield. I bring my knees to my chest and hug, tight, as I prepare to listen.

"Vivian, I need to tell you this. I tried to tell you this. Just...let me finish before you kick me out again, please," he pleads, a tear already falling down his cheek. I close my eyes, the sight of him crying sends a stinging pain to my heart. I swallow hard and let him speak.

"I was fifteen.." He trails with a shaky breath. "A couple of older kids were having a party. My brother begged me to go with him. It was a school night, but the home we were placed at didn't give a shit if we went to school or not. We were drinking and taking pills at the party. I don't know what I took; everyone kept handing me things, and I thought nothing of it. I was so fucked up by the time we got back into the car I passed out. I only woke up when my seat belt locked, and my whole body jerked. I was trying to figure out what had happened, but my eyes kept rolling back every time I tried to pay attention... I couldn't see straight. I saw a red car and a woman with brown hair. She had her head on the steering wheel to the side of us. Blood was running down her face. She looked...she looked like you did, Vivian."

His face grows more flushed, and his eyes well with more tears. I can hardly see him from the tears blurring *my* vision. He sits on the armrest of the opposite side as he continues. "I thought I was hallucinating. It was as if everything I was looking at was fake. It wasn't real. The next thing I know, I...I woke up on the Birch's lawn. They brought me inside, and I slept all day. I woke up on the fourth of July and went to look for my brother. Trying to make sense of what I saw. I found him a day later, under some bridge with a couple of other kids. He was high out of his mind. It was unlike him. He would drink and shit at parties, but he wasn't one to just take drugs regularly. I tried to have a conversation with him, but it went nowhere. I think it was the guilt or trauma that got to him. His drug use didn't stop, and when I realized that what I saw was not a hallucination, I went to the police station to report it, to report my brother. I didn't know the location or the time it was, and by then, there had already been over a hundred car accidents that had happened. I...I didn't speak to my brother since. I stopped taking pills, I..stopped doing any drugs. The last time I drank alcohol was my twenty-first birthday, and I just had one drink. We can go to the police, and I can tell them everything. I'm sorry, Vivian...I'm so sorry." His voice cracks at every sentence. As if this has been weighing on him for years. I sob into my sweatshirt. The tears from my eyes and mucus from my nose combining onto my sleeve. I don't know what to think. Somehow, what he said only leaves me with more questions.

"You weren't driving?" I ask in between heavy sobs.

"No, Vivian, I wasn't." He shakes his head slowly.

"How old was your brother?"

"He was sixteen."

"Your brother is...is dead?"

"Yes, Vivian."

I cry harder with my head down again, knowing that whatever punishment I was hoping for twelve years ago would never come.

"I...I just had to tell you. I'll go now. I'm so sorry." He sighs with pain in his voice.

I hear the shuffling of him standing from the armrest of the couch, taking a few steps before he pauses. "I have never felt this way about anyone in my life before. I love you, Vivian. If there is a chance, I could do something, *anything* to keep you...I'll do it. I swear to God I'll do whatever you need me to," he pleads quietly as I keep my head down.

His words collide in my head, one side fighting for love, the other fighting with anger. I hear his footsteps move slowly after some silence between us.

"I forgive you...both," I whisper, tears streaming down my face.

"Vivian," he sighs.

"I forgive you," I say more surly, tilting my head up so my eyes can meet his. His breathing shutters as he brings his hand to his mouth. I stand up and walk towards him.

"I can't," he whispers as he shakes his head *no.* "I could never forgive my brother."

"You have to, Matt," I say quietly, bringing my hand to the back of his arm. "You can't live with that much hate in your heart...and neither can I."

His eyes soften as he looks at me. I see him swallow hard as the air between us becomes less thick.

"I love you," he whispers as his forehead falls on mine. I swallow and lick my lips before speaking.

"I love you too, Matt." I breathe into his mouth. Our faces nearly touching.

He leans in, his lips only grazing against mine. We breathe into each other as I brush my top lip on his. He sighs slightly, and I brace myself to lean my face further into him, crashing my lips onto his as I take a heavy breath. He kisses me back as my hands thread the hair on the back of his head, and his hands fall to my waist. I sigh against his touch as his hand lightly traces along my spine, making his way to the top as he grips the back of my neck with pressure. I dive my tongue into his mouth as he flirts back with mine. I want him, *all* of him, right now.

"Shower?" I whisper when our lips part briefly.

I can feel a faint smile form on his lips as my eyes stay closed. He grabs my hand, and I follow him upstairs to my bathroom. He starts the water and lifts my sweatshirt up slowly. Landing his lips on mine after it's off. He grabs the side of my neck as his tongue touches my lips. I part my mouth slowly to let him in. He kisses me so passionately my head feels like it's swirling. As his mouth leaves mine, he grabs the hem of my T-shirt and lifts it over my head, diving his mouth to my neck. I moan as I feel his hot tongue gliding on my skin and his hand come up to cup my breast. He gently runs his thumb over my nipple and kisses my neck again, softly biting me as he goes in. He pushes himself between my legs a bit, his cock, rock solid against me.

As my fingers grip his hair, he moves his hands to my leggings, hooking them with his fingers and pulling them down. Releasing his mouth from my neck as he kneels before me. I stand, completely naked in front of him as he kisses my leg just above my knee. Higher and higher, he makes his way inside of my thigh, his bottom lip, wet from his tongue, gently caresses the outside of my pussy. I whimper as he teases me, and he does it again, slowly adding his tongue. He runs his tongue closer, so close it lightly grazes my clit. I moan, grabbing the back of his hair tightly. He kisses me again, then runs the flat of his tongue right on top of me, caressing my slit with the rigidness of his tongue and beard. I bury his face in me, using two hands on the back of his head. I grind my hips while I ride his face. He moans into me, and I whimper back. His tongue flicks at my clit as he alternates sucking on it, and his hands move from my hips to my ass as he squeezes, pulling me into him so he can taste me further.

I continue to grind on his tongue, pushing myself over the edge. I cry out as I come on his face, and he stands up, his beard and skin glistening with *me*. His cock bulges through his sweatpants so well I can see the thick outline of it from start to finish. He lifts up his shirt and tosses it to the floor before pulling down his sweatpants and boxers. His cock bounces from the pull of the clothing, and he moves towards me, picking me up with my legs wrapped around him. I grind my hips to stroke him up and down with my wet pussy, and he moans as his lips collide with mine. He walks us into the shower, and the hot water scolds my side as he pins me against the wall. He rubs his cock in between my legs, faster on my clit — edging me further until a mix between a cry and grunt escapes from my lips as I come again.

"I love you." He whimpers into my mouth, taking my lips with his again, pushing his tongue against mine as I fight to get inside his mouth. He moves his hips back to make himself straighter as he thrusts right into me. Pushing slowly. He angles his hips to get deeper inside of me while I groan against his mouth, parting my lips from his as I gasp for air. My cheek rests on the side of his face while I moan with every plunge into me. Slowly and deeply, he forces himself inside of me.

My legs squeeze tighter around him as he hunches over and pulls me away from the wall, putting his arms around my back to fuck me harder. Gravity swings my body against his, only making his cock go deeper and deeper inside of me. He grunts loudly as I cry out. He straightens up, lifting me off of him and turning me around. I brace my hands on the wall and arch my back as he slides into me slowly from behind. He grabs my hips and thrusts into me repeatedly, moving his hips to push deeper. I moan and push my hips against him, moving *faster* so he will. He groans as he slaps my ass. The sting sends a surge through my body, causing me to whimper.

I moan. "Harder."

He pushes harder into me as he slaps my ass again with more of a bite. He grips my hips firmly as he forces into me before releasing one hand to grasp my hair tightly. He wraps my locks around his fist as he pulls my body up with it. He fucks me harder as his mouth lands on my ear. His tongue grazes my earlobe as he bites gently. He pulls my hair back further to meet my mouth with his as he dives his tongue into me. I bite his bottom lip as his rhythm slows down, and he moans quietly with each deliberate plunge into me.

"I'm gonna come," he groans before only thrusting a couple more times before he pulls out and pushes my body around, signaling me to fall to me knees.

I open my mouth the second I kneel, stretching my tongue out with a smile, a smile that only forms from watching him stroke himself as his hot come falls on my tongue. He moans and whimpers as he finishes, and I wrap my mouth around him, making sure to suck every last drop there is. I swallow and taste him as I stand up. The taste, almost sour, like from dehydration. He pulls me into him as the water droplets ricochet off of us. I look up at him as he looks at me, his lips falling to mine gently. I turn us around, so my back is under the water. Running my hands through my hair to soak it. I look at Matt, his carved-out body, six or eight muscles in his stomach. I can't even focus on counting right now. The V line points directly to his perfect prized possession, which is still somewhat hard. I grab the shampoo and start to wash my hair as he grabs the body wash behind me and rubs it on himself. The suds press against his skin as he leans in to kiss me again, only parting my lips slightly with his. I rinse my hair out and grab the conditioner to lather it in while he washes *my* body next, moving his hands to my breasts and massaging them while he dips his tongue in my mouth, and I graze mine lightly against his. He bites my bottom lip softly as he moves his hands between my legs, bringing the body wash everywhere between me. Circling my clit lightly while his tongue still flirts with mine. I move my hand to his cock and stroke him gently, only griping mildly. I twist my wrist while I glide against him. He groans into me as he moves me under the water to rinse off before turning me around so he can do the same to himself. I keep stroking him until I feel his arms wrap around me, picking me up again to carry me out of the shower. He shuts the water off with one hand as he holds me in the other before he walks us out of the bathroom and tosses me on my bed.

He climbs on, as I prop myself up on my elbows to watch him. He lifts my hips as he guides himself inside of me, my pussy still soaking wet. He moves my legs higher as he plunges into me. Fucking me harder and harder as I moan. Our bodies slippery against each other from the shower. He grabs my hips with force as he pushes inside of me, pausing slightly every time I'm completely filled with him. He grunts and I observe his face — his mouth is dropped slightly while his eyebrows wrinkle. He looks at me with fire in his eyes as we lock our gaze. His lips curl up to a smile while his mouth was still parted as he thrusts into me faster.

"I'm coming," I cry out. I can feel his cock pulsing inside of me as he pushes in.

He moans as his mouth drops wider, watching my body react to him. He slows down, dropping my legs and cupping my head in his hands. His lips crash into mine while he thrusts slowly into me. My legs still parted to each side so I can be as open as possible for him. He grabs the back of my neck with one hand while his tongue and mine intertwine. I whimper against his mouth while I taste our breaths mixed together. His mouth pulls away from mine as our lips lightly rest together. Our breathing equally loud and shallow. He continues to move inside me, forcing his hips to push in deeper.

"I love you," I sigh against his lips. He lightly kisses me as his hips move faster. He bites my bottom lip gently and groans, pulling out of me quickly before he grabs his cock with his hand. He collapses slightly on me, and I feel his come drain between us.

He twitches slightly as he brings his face up to meet mine, kissing me gently once more. He rolls to the side of me, keeping me close in his arms. We lay for a moment, naked and pinned against one another, trying to calm our breathing. After a moment, he kisses the side of my head while his hand still forms around the back of my neck. I tilt my head against him and smile before slowly lifting up to go back into the bathroom and clean myself up. He follows after, and I grab a towel and wipe my stomach as he comes up behind me and kisses the top of my head, my hair still slicked back from the shower. I look up at him behind me and smile as I hand him the towel before I go to my closet and throw on an oversized T-shirt while finding one of Matt's sweatshirts he left here and tossing it to him as he exits the bathroom.

"I don't want to be apart from you, Vivian. Ever again, "he breathes into my ear after we get into bed, and I snuggle against him. "I can't imagine my life without you in it."

"I love you, Matt," I whisper with a smile as my eyes close. Before drifting to sleep, I feel his lips kiss the back of my head as he tucks me further inside his arms.

"I love you more, Vivian."

CHAPTER TWENTY-SEVEN

Nothing good ever comes from a late-night phone call, not in my experience, anyway. Matt left the room as I checked my phone to see the time. Two forty-two in the morning. I can hear him on the phone outside of the door as I try to listen.

Hospital, is all I heard.

Not unusual for Matt.

My eyes drift closed again.

"It's Bill," Matt announces loudly as he enters my bedroom.

"What?" I ask as I spring my eyes open. I flip the covers off of me as I see Matt put on his sweatpants.

"Caroline called the ambulance. Bill's not breathing. We're going to meet them at the hospital. She was going to call you next," he says as he puts his shoes on.

I stand there, taking it all in, my mind trying to catch up with his mouth. I spring towards my closet and throw on pants. We rush downstairs, and I grab a jacket on the way out, forgetting to even lock my door.

We run to Matt's car, parked down the street a bit, and were off as soon as we get in.

"Was the ambulance there already?" I ask with a heavy breath from running.

"It didn't sound like it," he says as he looks in his rear-view mirror to switch lanes.

I can't focus on anything else. Not the drive, not the roads, my eyes are shifted on Matt as he weaves in and out of traffic with ease. He pulls into the parking garage, and I don't wait for him to open my door for me. I'm out as fast as he is, following him through the hospital as he uses his key card to open doors. We make our way through the long hospital halls to the emergency waiting room.

"Caroline!" Matt shouts as he spots her following along-side paramedics. We move towards her as she pauses, her face red and eyes swollen. My eyes well with tears as I see her and see what looks to be Bill being pushed on a gurney through more doors.

"We can only allow family back there during this time," A doctor says to Matt and me.

"They are," Caroline retorts back to him. The doctor looks at Matt with familiarity in his eyes. He knows Matt, and he knows Matt doesn't have any family. The doctor nods as we three follow him behind the automatic doors. Caroline drops her eyes with sadness as she moves through. Matt and I follow closely behind.

We round the corner in the hallway as we come to a row of rooms. We follow the doctor into the second one and see three people around Bill. One crowded over him, performing CPR, while the other two open drawers and pull out different things. I hear them speak but don't understand. My ears become plugged as I watch. The only thing I can hear is Caroline's sobs.

Matt asks the doctor that brought us in if he can help. I didn't see what they said because my eyes are focused on Bill. He looks like he's sleeping, and the way they are pushing on his chest looks like it would hurt terribly. Caroline sits on a chair, wailing loudly, bringing her hands to her face. I sit next to her as Matt runs around the room, helping hand things to the nurses. The tears steadily flow down my cheeks. They work tirelessly on Bill with hard and fast compressions. I watch. Hoping and praying to whatever god will listen to keep Bill here, with us, just a little bit longer.

"Time of death..." The Doctor starts before Caroline's screaming becomes the only thing the entire room can hear.

I drop my head, my heart rate quickens as my breath grows rapidly, and the thought of him gone, actually gone, is sinking in. Matt stands there with a grim look on his face and his hands on top of his head. His posture slumps as he brings his hands to his face, crying audibly into them. Caroline keeps screaming, and my sobs grow louder over the two. I get off my chair to squat near Caroline, wrapping her in my arms as I cry into her sweater. She grabs my arm and hugs me tighter, screaming into mine. Matt towers over us, putting his arms around us as we wait for everyone to leave. As soon as they do — we help Caroline up to stand and walk toward Bill.

Matt and I sit while she holds his hand and whispers to him, gently placing a kiss on his forehead. She moves slightly, and I allow Matt to stand up first, letting him take the time he needs with Bill. He stands and extends his hand to me, wanting me to say goodbye to him. I don't hesitate. I grab his hand, and we walk to Bill together. I stand over him, looking at Bill with his eyes closed, his arms at his sides, and his skin mottled with light blue and purple hues. He's cold to the touch and already...I miss him. The tears fall from my face onto Bill's bed, and I silently tell him all of the things I wish I could have said to him one last time. *Thank you, Bill, for everything you've taught me. For bettering me as a person. For letting me win one time at poker. For telling me your secrets. For bringing me into your family like a granddaughter. Love always, Vivy.*

After Matt and I dropped Caroline off at home and stayed with her for a while, we finally arrived back at Matt's place around five in the morning. I lay here in bed, listening to him snore softly. I can't sleep. I should stay up anyway because I told Caroline I'd handle the store in the coming weeks. The last thing she needs to be doing is working. I've got to be at Birch Books in an hour and a half, so I decide to quietly get out of bed and head to Matt's kitchen. I make myself a cup of coffee and sit at his round dining table, taking the view of the city in as the sun rises. Sharp reds and oranges take over as the sun rises, and I cannot help but feel the warmth as I look at it. It's bright and lively, almost like fire with that perfect zip and effervescence.

Hi Bill.

I sit and watch as the bright colors slowly turn more muted, and the blue sky appears. I finish my coffee and quietly return to Matt's room, grabbing a t-shirt of his from the neatly folded stack in his closet and finding a pair of jeans I had left here previously. I quickly change and kiss Matt softly goodbye before heading downstairs and out the door to walk. It's quiet this morning, and the air presents a bitter chill now that fall is right around the corner. I arrive at Birch Books and unlock the front door with the key Caroline gave me hours ago.

Turning on each light as I walk through, I make my way back toward Bill's office. I turn on the light as I stand in the doorframe. I can picture him sitting there, reading. I smile faintly at the thought, but immediately my smile dissipates, realizing I won't ever see that sight again. Now, it is only a memory. A tear runs down my cheek as I turn the light back off. No sense in keeping it on when no one will be in there.

The day drags slowly as I tend to customers with as much of a smile as I can fake. I've checked in with Caroline twice today, and Matt said he was almost there to help her find pictures for Bill's funeral. I've already sent him a couple I had. One is a selfie of Bill and me that he insisted I take. He had his favorite sweater on that day, which was apparently Caroline's *least* favorite, so he wanted to text her a photo out of spite, loving spite, that is. The other picture I sent was one of Bill and Caroline, my personal favorite. After walking into the office multiple times and seeing Bill read to Caroline from across the desk, I finally snapped a secret photo. I showed them later, but it's one of my favorite memories of them—a perfect display of their love, in my opinion.

The hours move slowly as six o'clock rolls around. I swiftly close down and lock up, texting Matt as soon as I'm on the sidewalk.

Me: Are you still at Caroline's?
Matthew: Just about to leave. Want me to get dinner and come over?
Me: Please. See you soon

I arrive home at the same time Matt does. I always forget his driving is much faster than my slow walking. He picked up my favorite pasta from a small restaurant near his house. It's little things like that that make me fall more in love with him. The slight things he remembers, my likes and dislikes, and little bits of information show he truly listens. We dive into dinner while snuggling on the couch together when suddenly a knock comes on my front door. I snap my head to look, only to hear the knock once more. I swiftly move to the door and swing it open to see Lauren.

"I heard about Bill...I'm so sorry, Viv..." she says with saddened eyes as her gaze falls to her hands. I wrap her in my arms, hugging her tight. I haven't spoken to her since I yelled at her, and the emotions I have run through me like a tidal wave. I pull away from her slightly as I open the door further, exposing her sight to see Matthew sitting on the couch. She smiles with a closed mouth as her lips curl upward.

"I love you," I whisper to her with a smile. "Do you want some dinner?" I ask her quietly.

"No, oh my gosh, no, I just wanted to stop by and see you. I've got to get home. Call me tomorrow?" she says, her eyes still glossy.

I nod and hug her once more, telling her to text me once she's home. I shut the door and walk back to Matt, taking a closer seat. I'm not hungry anymore, and all I want to do is lay with him. As the night goes on, we move upstairs to get ready for bed. I climb in as he grabs a book from my nightstand.

"It's a new one we're thinking of adding to the store," I say as he reviews the back cover.

"Have you started it?" he asks with curiosity in his eyes.

I shake my head no with pursed lips as he climbs in bed next to me, opening the book to the first page. I move closer to him, tucking my arm into his as I lay my head on his shoulder.

His hand falls gently to my knee as he begins reading. "Above and behold, the darkest of my days that lie ahead…"

Matt reads as my body calms from the past twenty-four hours. I lie here with the man I love, our emotions completely stripped down from the last couple of days, listing to him as his thumb grazes over my leg, his hand only lifting from me to turn the page. Chapter after chapter, he reads to me softly and slowly as my eyes drift shut.

CHAPTER TWENTY-EIGHT

The past three weeks have been nothing short of chaotic. Matt and I mostly helped Caroline with paperwork, funeral planning, headstone choosing, and anything else she possibly needed us to do. It's strange without Bill. Especially at Birch Books. I've taken over these past weeks so Caroline could stay home. I find myself most days walking into Bill's office, just standing in the doorway, picturing him at his desk. I miss him, and I miss him calling me from the other room to help with silly little things. It doesn't get easier dealing with death. You would think I should be so experienced by now.

The bell above the door chimes and I glance up, my sight falling on Caroline as she walks in with an envelope in her hand.

"Hello, Vivy."

"Hi! I was going to come over after I closed up today."

"No need, hunny. You and Matt have done so much for me this past month, take some time and enjoy yourselves, don't worry about little ol' me," she says as she walks closer to me. "Let's go into the office. I have something for you."

We push through the curtain and walk in back to the office. Caroline takes a seat in Bill's chair, and I sit across from her. She adjusts the glasses on her nose before glancing at me.

"Over the years, Bill and I did many things together. Having children, though, was one thing we could not do. I know he's shared stories with you. But I feel you should know that Bill loved you very much...along with Matty. And the sight of you two together, I think it filled his heart well enough that he was finally ready to leave this earth," she says as her eyes become misty. "Well, I have this for you," she says as she hands me the white envelope.

I take it from her and hold it in front of me, my name, *Vivian*, written out in Bill's handwriting. My sight shifts to Caroline's eyes as a tear falls down her cheek. She nods as if for me to open it up here. I gently lift up the envelope flap and take out a folded piece of paper. I begin to read slowly.

Vivy, I first off would like to say thank you. The amount of joy you have brought into Caroline and my life just by being in it is simply unmatched. Your kindness, your drive, and your hardworking attitude are just some of the things we love most about you. As my health declines, I feel it's very important to have proper precautions and measures in place so Caroline will not have to worry, should I go first. Both Caroline and I have discussed this decision deeply, and while it does not come lightly, we do not want you to feel pressured. I don't see why someone like you shouldn't have everything and more they've ever dreamed of, so that's why we have decided to name you Vivian Westwood as the new proud owner of Birch Books. We know you will take great care of it, and there is no other person in the world we would see fit to run it. Of course, only when Caroline is ready to let go. I know you're scared, Vivy, but be afraid — and do it anyway.

Love ya, Bill.

P.S. I didn't let you win that hand of poker. You did that all yourself. Always proud of you, kiddo.

As my crying subsides when I finish the letter, I look at Caroline over the top of the paper to see the tears falling from her eyes.

"I'm ready now," she says as she shakes her head up and down. "I'm ready for you to take over, sweetheart, only if you want to. I know this is a lot. Take a day or so to think about it, okay?" she says with a pressed smile through her tears.

I'm in shock, utter shock. My pulse grows rapidly, and I need to deeply breath three or four times. I shake my head yes as a laugh comes out, and a large smile forms on my face as the tears fall.

"Yes, I will," I say with one more laugh, my tears falling from both happiness and grief. Caroline smiles as her tears fall, and she stands up. I stand with her to meet on the side of the desk and hug her tightly.

"Thank you," I whisper. She gives me one last squeeze before releasing me from her grasp.

"We will have our lawyer draw up the paperwork this week. I'm proud of you, Vivy. Also, how do you and Matty feel about dinner every Sunday? I'll cook for you kids, and make sure to make extra for your lunches the next day. How does that sound?" she says while holding on to both of my arms and standing directly in front of me.

"That sounds perfect, Caroline," I say with a smile. I hug her once more before we walk to the front together. She leaves, and I make my way toward the back, looking into Bill's office for the last time... the last time before it becomes *my* office. I smile with a warmness in my heart at the almost bittersweet feeling of joy washing over me. I return to the front counter to grab my phone and send Matt a quick text.

Me: Can you come to the store around 7?
Matthew: Absolutely.

As closing time rolls around, I switch the door sign and lock up, heading to the convenience store down the street. I grab a bottle of sparkling champagne, alcohol-free, and two plastic champagne flutes. I make my way back to Birch Books and let myself in, locking the door behind me. I walk straight behind the curtain and shut down all of the lights in the back before I make my way to the front, shutting off the large overhead lights and leaving the tall floor lamp on. I pour the sparking champagne into the flutes and set them on the end table near the lamp and oversized chair. I fix the books on the large table, straightening them out as I take a step back and look around *my* bookstore.

The overflow of books throughout is my favorite part. With the dim lighting now, it's peaked with coziness.

A knock comes from the front door, and I turn around quickly. Seeing Matt peer through the glass, bundled up in a long black jacket. I open the door and smile as he walks in. His facial features scream confusion as he walks further in and sees the flutes. I bend slightly to pick them up, handing a glass to him.

"What's this for?" he says with a puzzled grin.

"I thought you might like to have a drink with the new owner of Birch Books." I clink his glass with mine and take a sip.

His mouth drops in awe as the corner of his lips curl in a smile. He stands there, stunned. A chuckle comes out of his mouth as his smile grows bigger.

"Are you serious?" he asks.

I nod my head, yes, and before I know it, his glass is on the table, and his arms are around me, picking me up and twirling me, right in the center of the store. My champagne nearly spills out of the glass as we spin. We laugh together as he sets me down and firmly presses his lips on mine.

For once in my life, I feel whole.

I feel *complete*.

Life is full of unexpected challenges, decisions to make, and heartbreaking truths to learn—eventually, fate steps in. Putting you on the path you're destined to be, my path... just became incredibly clear.

ACKNOWLEDGMENTS

From the bottom of my heart, a huge thank you to my friends and family - the ones who have supported me from the beginning. Thank you for reading my very janky manuscript and giving me your honest opinions. Thank you to Rachel McEwan for the cover design, leaving me completely blown away after just the first draft. Thank you to the countless people I had read, review, and soft edit for me. To my developmental and line editors, Erin and Paige a very special thank you for not making me look like an idiot with grammar mistakes. Thank you to my husband, and my children for being so supportive throughout this entire venture. My daughter, Payton — I'm so sorry you can't read this book right now...give it ten more years until I'll be comfortable enough for you to read this story, but for now, my precious child...let's stick to your young adult

— very clean, books. To Brooke, the first person who knew I was going to write a novel, To Dani, the first person who read my novel, and to my mother, Arlene, thank you for still not speaking about the sex parts with me...it's really appreciated. Each of you played a huge role in my thought process with this story and I couldn't possibly have enough words to tell you how grateful and thankful I am for each of you. With all this being said, it has been a wild and fun ride...and I can't wait for the next chapter this journey has to offer.

ABOUT AUTHOR

Madeline Flagel is a mom with two kids who are in every sport imaginable. So while free time is sparse, she does enjoy reading and travel. She's a beach bum, Chicago Cubs fan, and an entrepreneur, starting and selling many companies throughout her career. Madeline is an avid reader of romance novels and an even spicier writer of the genre. *How Often We Collide* is her debut novel, and she is thrilled to release it to the world.